Rutland Library Services
www.rutland.gov.uk/libraries

Rutland
County Council

MURDER IN THE FOURTH ROUND

IAN SIMPSON

Matador
9 Priory Business Park,
Wistow Road, Kibworth Beauchamp,
Leicestershire. LE8 0RX
Tel: 0116 279 2299
Email: books@troubador.co.uk
Web: www.troubador.co.uk/matador
Twitter: @matadorbooks

ISBN 978 1788037 419

British Library Cataloguing in Publication Data.
A catalogue record for this book is available from the British Library.

Printed and bound in the UK by TJ International, Padstow, Cornwall
Typeset in 12pt Minion Pro by Troubador Publishing Ltd, Leicester, UK

Matador is an imprint of Troubador Publishing Ltd

*For Tara Wigley; if I am able to write fiction
it's thanks to her*

And

In memory of Willie Waterston (1949-2016).

Other books in the Flick and Baggo series:

Murder on Page One:

'Ian Simpson is a real find. *Murder on Page One* is a beautifully crafted, gripping piece of crime fiction that holds the attention from page one until the very end.' – *Alexander McCall Smith.*

Murder on the Second Tee:

'An engrossing mystery.' – *The Herald*;
'An entertaining police procedural and full of well-drawn characters … recommended.' – *Eurocrime*;

'Definitely a series to watch out for from a new talent on the crime writing scene.' – *Crime Fiction Lover.*

Murder in Court Three:

'Fabulously readable.' – *AustCrimeFiction*;

'We await the fourth title of this engaging series with avid interest.' – *University of Edinburgh Journal.*

Also by Ian C Simpson,
the Sheriff Hector Drummond stories:

Sons of the Fathers
The Andrean Project

'Reputation is an idle and most false imposition; oft got without merit, and lost without deserving.'
William Shakespeare, Othello, Act II, Scene 3

Characters you will meet, and those associated with them:

The police:

Detective Inspector Flick Fortune
Detective Inspector Fergus Maxwell, her husband, based in Dundee
Verity Maxwell, their daughter
Bernard and Agnes Maxwell, Fergus' parents
Detective Sergeant Bagawath Chandavarkar (Baggo), Serious Fraud Office, Edinburgh
Melanie Arbuthnot, Advocate, Baggo's partner
Sheriff Charles and Cynthia Arbuthnot, Melanie's parents
Detective Constable Billy Di Falco
Detective Constable 'Spider' Gilsland
Constable Alex McKellar
Detective Sergeant Lance Wallace
Constable Dennis Austin

The 'Jolly Boys':

Tony Spencer, partner in L & P Campbell, Solicitors, Cupar, (murdered in 1984)

Mary Spencer, his widow

Peter Waldron, partner in Cradock Gill and Murdoch, Solicitors, St Andrews (convicted of Spencer's murder)

Amy Smith, his daughter

Cammy Smith, his son-in-law

Sandy Smith, his grandson

Joss Montpellier, partner in Montpellier and Montpellier WS, Solicitors, St Andrews (retired)

Georgia Montpellier, his wife

David Montpellier, their son

James Lightbody, partner in Reid and Fanshawe, Solicitors, Crail

Norma Lightbody, his wife

Hugh Harkins, partner in Cradock Gill and Murdoch, Solicitors, St Andrews

Susan Harkins, his wife and ex-wife of Peter Waldron

Kevin McPhail, owner of East Neuk Properties Ltd

Linda McPhail, his second wife

The Others:

Noel Osborne, ex-Detective Inspector in the Metropolitan Police (Inspector No)

Eric Cox, a political activist

Mrs Rosaleen Cox, his mother

Dr MacGregor, a pathologist

Dino Rizzoli, Chip Shop owner, St Andrews

Amanda, a waiter in the Adamson Restaurant

Francis Thomson, Detective Sergeant (retired)
Martin Silver, a jogger
Harriet Cowan, a procurator fiscal depute, who prosecutes
Mrs Elizabeth McNaughton, former secretary to Joss Montpellier
Heather Fabroni, formerly cash room clerk in L & P Campbell
Hamish Murray, Justice of the Peace, St Andrews

PROLOGUE
St Andrews, 22nd July 1984

The murder weapon was a wooden golf tee. It had splintered and the point had broken off, leaving the stem a thin, sharp sliver of wood. This had been coated with Batrachotoxin, extracted from the skin of the Golden Poison Dart Frog and used by Columbian natives to lethal effect.

Tony Spencer hardly felt the scratch on his bare arm. For one thing, he was very drunk. For another, the fourth round of the Open Championship was reaching a dramatic climax in front of him. Standing on the mound behind the seventeenth, the famous Road Hole, he shuffled and wriggled among the excited spectators. Everyone wanted to get simultaneously a view of Tom Watson, a few yards away, assessing an impossibly difficult shot hampered by the wall bounding the course, and Severiano Ballesteros, stalking a birdie putt on the distant eighteenth green. Playing briskly as usual, Watson managed to scuffle his ball onto the narrow seventeenth green but a long way from the pin. Ahead, several thousand people held their breath as Ballesteros putted. His ball hovered on the lip before dropping in. He punched the air repeatedly and the crowd roared their approval. Watson missed his putt for a par and the Championship was as good as over.

Despite his fuddled state, Tony Spencer could feel that something was wrong. The poison was in his bloodstream, attacking his nervous system and his heart. Within minutes he was writhing on the ground. Before Ballesteros signed his winning scorecard, he was dead.

1

St Andrews, August 2015

'Here's another doctor who says there's no risk of him doing a Megrahi and living for years rather than months. "Waldron's pancreatic cancer is likely to cause death within a month or two and no period of respite can be anticipated."' Amy Smith looked up from the sheaf of Scottish Prison Service papers that had thudded through the letter-box, disturbing breakfast. 'They're only letting him out because he's dying. You really don't need to worry,' she told her husband.

Cammy Smith said nothing and continued to concentrate on getting as much of a banana into Sandy as the two-year-old would allow.

'He could be here as soon as Friday,' she added. 'If we're to say no, we have to do it now.' She watched Cammy grimace and wished he would speak his mind so she could counter his objections. But her father had caused more arguments between them than any other issue; she understood why he was treading carefully. 'Please, Cammy, cards on the table. I can't bear it when you fester.'

Cammy put down the banana and said carefully,

'They've kept him locked up for thirty-one years, yet most murderers get out after a dozen. He's killed two people. They must reckon he's dangerous or he'd have been out years ago. How's he going to behave? How is he going to be with the wee guy? Will he have his criminal mates coming to visit him?'

Amy felt like screaming but managed to keep her voice level. How many times had she been forced to defend her father? 'He didn't play the system. He has never accepted he was guilty of Spencer's killing. And when the parole board chairman asked what he would do if he found out who had framed him, he said he would kill them. And they took it seriously. You know that. The other murder was a child molester and he felt he had to join in with the rest of the prisoners. He only gave him a few kicks. It was the kicks the pervert got from the rest that killed him. But Father had to carry the can for the rest.' She reached for Cammy's hand, leathery, chaffed and strong. 'Darling, I've been visiting him and I'm sure he'll be fine. You've met him only once. And it'll be me who'll have to cope with any problems. He'll stay with us for a few weeks then go into hospital at the end.' She paused. 'If I don't take him in now, I know I'll regret it.' Her voice caught.

She was shaking. Having a convicted murderer as her father had moulded her life. Over the years she had developed a thick skin and an abrupt manner to shield her from cruel barbs, subtle or blatant. She had stopped caring that many people in St Andrews thought she was rude and chippy. She had no time for those with social pretensions and deliberately spoke with a stronger Scottish accent than she had as a child. The fact that Cammy was a plumber, a straightforward guy with the very ordinary name of Smith, rather than a lawyer or a doctor, had been a plus from the moment she had met him. Now that his business made more money than most solicitors, she was proud of him and didn't try to hide it.

Far from his emotional comfort zone, he stared out of the window, his desire not to upset Amy in conflict with the instinct to protect his family. 'What happens if we take him but he's impossible? Can we send him back?' he asked.

'I don't believe that will happen, but yes. He has to stay in approved accommodation and if we withdrew our consent to him living here, in the absence of somewhere else suitable, he'd be sent back to jail.'

That was something. A resigned grin on his face, he gripped her hand. 'All right. As it's really important to you, we'll do it.'

She got up and kissed his forehead. 'I love you, Cammy Smith,' she said, making him feel much better.

Sandy banged the tray of his high chair. 'Mama, nana,' he shouted, pointing to the mushy remnants of his breakfast.

* * *

Over the following days Amy had meetings with police, prison officials, social workers and nurses.

5

Her house was subject to intrusive inspection and there were times she was made to feel she was doing something wrong, particularly when a journalist tried to interview her. She was glad Cammy was out at work. It would all have been enough to put him right off the idea.

At half past eleven on the Friday after Cammy had agreed to the proposal, Peter Waldron arrived at his daughter's home in an ambulance. The house was situated at the east end of South Street in St Andrews and was part of a terrace of large properties built in medieval times, the grey stones reputedly removed from the ruins of the nearby Cathedral. The front door led straight out to the street, which was busy with shoppers and tourists. One arm linked with a male nurse's, the other using a hospital-issue stick, Waldron walked unsteadily across the pavement towards the front door. He paused and inhaled deeply. 'Free air,' he said to no one in particular. A shout of 'Peter' made him turn his head and a camera flashed. The photographer seemed to have appeared from nowhere. Waldron waved his stick at him, nearly over-balancing and causing the nurse to tighten his grip on his arm. Beside the photographer, a scruffy-looking woman with long, grey hair and a centre parting held up a placard, LIFE SHOULD MEAN LIFE. There was a younger man beside her. He had round spectacles, shiny hair and an angry expression. A classic 'young fogey' in cavalry twill trousers and a tweed jacket with a red, white and blue bow tie, he carried a placard with the same message. The camera flashed again and the nurse tried to pull Waldron towards the house but he resisted.

'Do you deserve a sympathetic release? Are you still a danger?' a thin-faced man with a notebook shouted.

'I am innocent,' Waldron spat at them, 'and I'm going to prove it.'

'You should still be locked up,' the young fogey shouted in a patrician, anglified voice.

Waldron stood defiantly, glaring at the crowd that was forming as Amy and the nurse tried to drag him inside. He lacked the strength to resist for long and they got him in then slammed the door. The family dog, Benjy, sniffed at him doubtfully.

'I want to tell my story,' Waldron said.

Amy forced herself to stay calm. She knew she had to establish who was in charge. 'No, Father, you can't. You're not allowed to speak to the press. It's one of the conditions of your release. They'd twist it anyway.' She led him to the back of the house and into the ground floor room she had prepared for him. It was light and sunny, with a large open window through which the scent of flowers wafted from the garden. He showed scant interest in the en suite bathroom that she had taken great care over, equipped as it was with grab rails and a mobile shower seat. He sat on the bed frowning, as the nurse carried in his battery of pills followed by several polythene bags full of books, notes and documents, and finally some clothes and a wheelchair.

Refusing Amy's offer of tea or coffee, the nurse

and the ambulance driver left. When they came to say goodbye to him, Waldron ignored them.

Amy thanked them as she saw them out. 'Good luck with him,' the nurse muttered.

Slowly, she walked back to her father's room. He had not moved and barely looked up when she came in.

This was the man who was her biological father. She had no awareness of having been in the same household. Only four when he had been taken away, she had no memory of that beyond seeing her mother cry for the first time. She had not known that big people sometimes did cry. She had always realised that Hugh Harkins, who had married her mother when she was six, was not her real father. He had wanted her to call him 'Dad' but she had resisted, inventing a name, 'H-man', for him. H-man and her mother had 'protected' her from her own father throughout her rebellious childhood, but at age eighteen she had visited Peter Waldron. The days for calling him 'Dad' were past, and she was not going to call him 'Peter' or 'Waldron', so 'Father' he was.

She thought she had got to know him over the last seventeen years but suddenly she doubted it. His grey complexion had seemed natural in jail, but here, in her cheerful home, it was as if death itself had come calling. Like her he was tall but, while she held herself straight, he stooped badly. They both had ski-jump noses and dark eyes unusually wide apart. The genetic link was obvious, but this man seemed so out of place that to her he was like an alien. And the unexpected reception committee had left her shaken. Might Cammy's fears have been well-founded? What would he say when he heard what had happened?

'Would you like to see round the garden?' she asked hesitantly.

'Yes,' he said and pushed himself up off the bed. He took his stick in one hand and her arm in the other and allowed himself to be guided round, Benjy snuffling behind them. 'I can walk with a stick if someone takes my arm,' he explained.

'Are you in pain?' she asked.

'Mercifully, no. But I have no energy.'

'That's understandable.' With the enthusiasm of a keen gardener, Amy described the variety of flowers coming into bloom in the secluded walled garden accessed by a door beside his room. His responses were taciturn and he seemed more interested in the ancient, seven-foot stone walls than in the plants. When she told him the huge, spreading yew tree in the middle of the garden probably dated from the days of King Robert the Bruce he nodded brusquely. Benjy lifted his leg against it proprietorially. With the front end of a medium-sized terrier and the back end of something quite big and hairy, Benjy was an unusual looking dog, rescued from the Dog and Cat Home and now a devoted pet. His front legs were shorter than his back legs so when he peed his long spine twisted precariously and he sometimes overbalanced. He did so this time. Waldron merely looked bemused.

The horticultural tour over, Amy quickly showed him round the ground floor then left him to unpack. She hesitated before phoning Cammy on his mobile, but reckoned he should hear about the demonstration from her. He answered quickly but paused before responding, sounding anxious as he sought reassurance that she was all right.

'Don't worry,' she told him. 'It's just a storm in a tea-cup.' But the morning's events had shaken her, and she knew he would realise that.

Just after one, she went to fetch her father for lunch to discover him asleep, the clean bedspread smeared with earth from his shoes. He had been provided with ill-fitting clothes; she would have to buy him better ones, a complete wardrobe. Worse, despite the open window, she caught a whiff of disinfectant and male sweat which she remembered from her prison visits. She shuddered then said loudly, 'Father, time for lunch'. She had planned a special meal to get the stay off to a good start, but it was with a sinking heart that she waited for him in the kitchen, which was opposite his room. She knew there had been a Peter Waldron who had been good fun and enjoyed life, but he had been hard to find over recent years and it looked as if now he had gone for good.

She heard the toilet flush and a short time later he wheeled himself in, deftly manoeuvring himself to the place set for him at the oak table.

'Some wine as it's a bit of an occasion?' she asked hopefully.

For the first time since his arrival, he smiled.

'We're having lemon sole as a main course but I thought you might like a red Bordeaux?'

He reached for the bottle which Amy had opened earlier and examined the label. '1998 Chateau Haut-Franquet I see. Excellent! It knows what it is to be kept inside for a long time.' His face lit up as he poured himself some and inhaled the bouquet. 'A hint of what? Yes, bramble,' he murmured, gently swilling the wine round the neglected crystal Amy had got out specially. In an instant, the surly ex-con was replaced by a wine connoisseur. His nose still in his glass, he began to croon indistinctly. Amy recognised the words as French. 'Chevaliers de la table ronde, goutons voir si le vin est bon.' After repeating this, he sipped the wine and held it in his mouth, savouring it before swallowing. 'You hang onto things, you know,' he said. 'At nights, surrounded by the noises and smells of prison, I forced myself to imagine I was tasting a fine wine. I'd almost given up hope of ever doing so again.' He took another sip and smiled. 'C'est bon,' he said. 'Tell me though, most people would not serve claret with sole. Why are you?'

The taste of wine was not the only thing he had held onto. He still spoke correctly, like the solicitor he had been, with less of a Scottish accent than Amy had developed. His dark, intelligent eyes were on her, expecting an answer to his question. 'Because the line that you should drink only white wine with fish is a wine snob's affectation. You told me that on one of my early visits to you.'

'Did I?' He smiled wistfully and took a bigger mouthful of wine. 'There was a time when I dared to hope. The Scottish Criminal Case Review Commission were taking me seriously. I allowed myself to remember the life I had, that I wanted to go back to. It became increasingly painful.'

Amy began to relax; he was communicating. The taste of wine had unlocked his inner self. 'I remember those early visits well. You had some great stories. I enjoyed them.'

'But you didn't enjoy the recent visits.' It was a statement, not a question.

Unsure how to respond, Amy nodded. 'First we have chicken soup,' she said, watching him drain his glass. She poured the soup into bowls she remembered using as a child, again brought out in the hope of making her father feel at home.

Waldron ate slowly and methodically, finishing what was put in front of him and applauding Amy's cooking, in particular not over-grilling the sole. He also drank most of the bottle of wine. Increasingly mellow, he described meals he had enjoyed before his arrest at restaurants now mostly closed or under different management. His face lit up as he recalled her, as a toddler, pouring salt into the pepper pot in the Old Course Hotel.

'It's very good now,' she said with a grin.

'The head waiter wasn't pleased.' He paused. 'I was proud of you.'

'So I get my cussedness from you?'

'Where else? I never greatly bothered what other people thought.'

'Cammy keeps saying it's in my DNA.'

They shared a moment of silence then he said, 'My office was just across the street. I see it's a cafe now.'

'They claim to serve the best coffee in St Andrews, but they don't,' she replied, smiling.

'How did you come to be in this house?'

She hesitated. During her prison visits she had prattled on about her and Cammy and Sandy and Benjy, avoiding mention of her mother and the man who had taken her father's place. And he hadn't asked. 'Mum and H-man bought this house soon after their marriage. A couple of years ago they decided to down-size, though actually they needed to free up some capital as the firm was struggling. Cammy and I put in an anonymous offer that was accepted.'

He nodded. 'Is Harkins still working?'

'Yes. He talks about retiring but I don't think he can afford to. They don't talk about it, but I believe something went wrong with his pension. He's developed a dreadful twitch. And he's bald now.'

He smiled and raised his eyebrows. 'You said the firm was struggling?'

'Yes. It's regarded as old-fashioned. The law's changed since your day. Even I know that but H-man isn't one to move with the times. They had to move to a smaller office. In Greyfriars Gardens.' Her father had built the firm up. She waited for some reaction but there was none.

'How's your mother?' He looked directly at her. It was the first time in many years he had mentioned her to Amy.

'She's well. Getting older, obviously. Has a bit of arthritis. They have a flat on The Scores. She plays a lot of bridge. And her garden's small but beautiful.' Gardening was the one enthusiasm Amy had inherited from her mother.

Her father said nothing but curled his lip contemptuously.

She decided not to beat about the bush. 'Tell me, do you resent H-man? He finished up with your business and your wife.'

He set down his glass with a bang. The frowning ex-con was back and Amy mentally kicked herself. 'And you. Of course I resent him, but I've no reason to think he framed me, and I've never rated him. But why make your offer for this house anonymous?'

'Cammy is a plumber. His business makes more than most lawyers these days, but the lawyers look down their noses on him. Doctors and academics too. The false smiles at our wedding were unbelievable. We wanted everyone to know we were buying this house with money Cammy has made, not as a family deal.' He raised his eyebrows. She couldn't stop herself from blurting out, 'It hasn't been easy, growing up as your daughter, and I'm sick of all snobs, social or wine.'

'Well thank you for sticking by me.' He smiled but said it lightly.

'It was a point of honour. I've always held my head up in this town and I don't mean to stop now.'

The conversation had gone places neither of them had expected it to go. Amy looked at the man who had made her life so difficult. She thought she saw a sense of entitlement and it made her mad. She broke the silence that followed. 'Well, Father, what's on your bucket list?' she asked abruptly, pouring the last of the wine into her own glass to prevent him from making himself sick.

'Bucket list? What do you mean?'

'Things you really want to do – before you die.' She looked in his eyes and saw no fear. 'Like climbing a particular mountain. Or bungee jumping,' she added lamely.

He reached over the table and took her hand in his. 'My dear, I hope I can call you that, there is one thing and one thing only that I intend to do, and that is prove my innocence. I did not kill Spencer, and with your help I mean to get justice for myself and those who believe in me.'

The words *with your help* caused her stomach to clench. This was something she hadn't bargained for. She looked round the room and saw the time. 'Heavens, I must pick up Sandy from his nursery. You'd best go to your room and have a wee sleep after all that wine.'

Laboriously, he wheeled himself back from the table. 'That was very good. Thank you,' he said, his voice slurred. 'Oh by the way,' he added, 'I want you to take me shopping for clothes. And would you be able to get me a decent-looking stick? I hate the one they gave me. It's so institutional.' Before she could reply, he wheeled himself out and the door of his bedroom slammed shut. She waited for a minute in the hall. In the absence of any crashes or bangs she assumed he had got safely onto his bed. Crunching a peppermint and only a minute or two late, she walked the short distance to Sandy's nursery, where he went three days a week. It was disconcerting to see the grey-haired woman who looked like a witch still holding her placard but now on the opposite side of the street. Amy realised she was Mary Spencer, widow of the man her father was said to have murdered. She had put on weight and lost pride in her appearance. Amy hadn't seen her for several years and believed she had left town.

Half an hour later, with Sandy down for his afternoon nap, Amy looked back on that challenging lunch. She found herself thinking of *A Tale of Two Cities*, a book that had resonated with her despite being forced to read it as a schoolgirl. Like Dr Manette, after years in prison, her father had been 'recalled to life'. Ironically, he had been recalled to life by imminent death. Amy imagined him sitting in his room, hammering away obsessively, making shoes like the doctor. It was better that he should spend whatever time he had left drinking fine wine. But she was unused to lunchtime alcohol, and suddenly felt very sleepy …

2

Flick Maxwell was driving away from the nursery from where she had picked up fourteen-month-old Verity when she spotted a grey-haired woman with a placard on South Street. It said something about life, but she thought little of it until she was home and changing a nappy. Her *alter ego*, Detective Inspector Flick Fortune, not long back from maternity leave, had received notice that a local murderer, Peter Waldron, was going to get a sympathetic release from his life sentence as he was dying of pancreatic cancer. There was a possibility of a hostile demonstration. The move had been criticised by Eric Cox, a right-wing Scottish politician who campaigned against the early release of prisoners. He would find out about particular releases then approach the victims or their relatives and orchestrate protests. He planned to stand against the Justice Secretary in the next Scottish elections and some commentators gave him a slight hope of success. Flick suspected that he was behind the woman with the placard in South Street.

A few hours later the Scottish television news proved her correct. His oiled hair immaculate but his face contorted with indignation, dark eyes blazing behind round frames, Cox stood in South Street and castigated the Justice Secretary for 'another spineless demonstration that the important people in the criminal justice system are the criminals and victims don't count.'

Flick took an instant dislike to him. The Scots were liable to associate her South of England accent with faux-posh speech like his. And he looked like someone who would run a mile rather than confront a violent criminal himself. More significantly, his inflammatory language was calculated to stir up emotions and cause unrest. She phoned Alex McKellar, who had been a constable in St Andrews 'since Young Tom Morris was in short troosers', as he told visiting golfers who had drunk too much. As she expected, he had observed Waldron's arrival from a discreet distance.

'It wis just hot air, ma'am. A bit of noise before Waldron went inside then a TV interview and Cox was away. The woman with him stayed. She's the widow of the man who was murdered. She wanted to block the Smiths' doorstep but I moved her across the street.'

'Yes, I saw her there. Did she seem likely to cause trouble, do you think?'

'Don't know, ma'am. By herself, probably not, but Cox can get people riled up, and the press have taken an interest, so I guess he'll be back.'

'Do you know much about Waldron? He killed another prisoner in jail, I think.'

'A child molester. A crowd of them did it, I believe,

but the rest were canny enough not to leave evidence. Waldron probably got involved to prove himself. The stupid bastard didn't clean the blood out of the seams of his shoes so he got convicted. The murder that took him to jail was different. I remember it well, as I was quite new here. He and the victim, Spencer, were both solicitors. There was a group of them, known as 'The Jolly Boys', solicitors, most of them. On the last day of the Open they'd all had a boozy lunch courtesy of a property company one of them owned. As Seve holed the winning putt, Waldron scratched Spencer's arm with a golf tee coated with poison from some South American frog. He died then and there. Waldron kept rare frogs as pets, including the one that killed Spencer, we found the tee in his pocket and he virtually admitted it.'

'My briefing said he had persisted in denying his guilt.'

'That's right, ma'am. He claimed he'd been verballed.'

Flick winced. She would not tolerate what were called 'old-fashioned methods' and wished she could see McKellar's face; his voice gave nothing away. 'Was there a motive?'

'For a wee while there had been a rumour that Spencer had been seeing Waldron's wife. It was the talk of the steamie here for weeks.'

Coming from the South of England, Flick was developing an understanding of Scottish colloquialisms and 'the talk of the steamie', meaning common gossip, was one of her favourites. 'Did Waldron know about it?' she asked.

'He did. It was a premeditated murder, but a crime of passion at the same time.'

'Thanks, Alex, that's very helpful. Keep an eye on things and don't hesitate to let me know if I can help. Oh, by the way, have you thought any more about what I said to you the other day?'

'Yes, I have, ma'am. Thank you, but I'm just not sure.'

'Well speak to someone, Lance Wallace perhaps. We both rate you highly, you know.'

When the young English woman, promoted to detective inspector and pregnant, had arrived in Fife, the experienced McKellar had treated her with contempt. She tried not to rise to this but, playing the long game, sought his view on local issues and gave him more respect than he gave her. As he came to realise she was more than the modern face of policing but was good at her job and not in the habit of throwing her weight around, his views and methods changed and now they were threatening to become a mutual admiration society. A few days earlier she had suggested he might like to end his career with a sergeant's stripes on his arm, but he liked his life as it was and did not want to contemplate the ignominy of failure.

Flick switched off her phone, glad that McKellar had a safe pair of hands and the knack few young officers had of defusing an awkward situation with some well-chosen words.

* * *

'You're not to stir things up by asking questions. It could get dangerous,' Cammy Smith hissed at Amy. Leaving Waldron downstairs in front of the television, they had gone together to bath Sandy, who had been embarrassingly wary of his grandfather.

'I see your point,' Amy said. They had seen Cox's performance on the Scottish News and had admitted to each other that they were apprehensive about future protests. 'But look, Father is determined to prove his innocence and I want to have someone on our side if these people start getting nasty. I went online before you got in, and I think I've found just the man to help us. He's very experienced in dealing with violent thugs. Hang on.' She left Cammy and Sandy playing with a rubber duck and returned with her i-pad. 'Look.'

Cammy dried his hands then read aloud. '"Ex-Detective Inspector Noel Osborne is a Rolls Royce among private eyes. After a career in which he cleaned up violent gang crime in the East End of London, and which ended with the solving of the literary agent murders, Noel is available for hire. As a private eye he has helped both his clients and the police. Notable cases in which he has played a crucial role have included the Bucephalus Bank murders in St Andrews and the Edinburgh Law Courts murder. Detection with discretion are his watchwords. He is

the man you want on your side." You want to hire him? How much does he cost? But this can't be him.'
He pointed to a photograph on the webpage showing a fat, red-faced man with a leery grin.

'I know it's not flattering, but it's not a beauty parade. I actually phoned the number on the page and spoke to him. His terms would be a thousand pounds for seven days in St Andrews.' She ignored her husband's wince. 'Plus air fares, as he lives in Spain, and bed and breakfast in a decent hotel, not the Old Course, for some reason he didn't explain. Come on, we could afford it, Cammy. I'd spend my savings on getting him. This is a world we don't know. We need help. And, and ...'

'And?'

'Why should Father go on and on about his innocence when he doesn't have long to live? Look, I believe him when he says he was framed. If we could prove that, he would die happy. At least we should try.'

Cammy shook his head. He could not tell if the dampness on her cheek came from the bath or her eye. His misgivings had been right but she was committed. If he didn't support her when she felt she needed it, their relationship would suffer. 'All right. I'll phone him now,' he said and went to the phone in their bedroom.

Ten minutes later he found her in Sandy's room, singing softly. He had not known what to expect of Osborne, but he supposed that a lot of private detectives sounded on the phone like Cockney wide boys. Cammy whispered to Amy, 'He's not impressive when you talk to him, is he? He speaks like someone out of *Only Fools and Horses*. I've asked for references and he'll e-mail them.'

She smiled. Sandy was asleep. 'I'm sure he's our man, darling. He seemed really keen to help us.'

Cammy knew some useless plumbers who were really keen to get jobs but didn't share the thought with Amy.

Over dinner Waldron said little but ate what had been put in front of him, first the cold ham, then the new potatoes, smothered in mayonnaise, then the salad. He purred when Amy produced a slab of Stilton and devoured a generous amount on well-buttered digestives, washing it all down with as much Chianti as Cammy was prepared to pour into his glass.

Cammy had a long-established arrangement to meet friends for pints of beer that evening. As he was preparing to leave, Osborne's e-mail arrived. His references comprised newspaper clippings testifying how bravely and cleverly he had outfaced criminals in London during his time in the police, then how much help the retired detective inspector had given former colleagues in complex investigations in St Andrews and Edinburgh. Critical examination would have shown that Osborne himself had contributed a number of quotes, but Cammy could tell Amy was determined to have him and they could afford a couple of weeks of his time. And he was desperate to get to the pub and drown his sorrows with his friends. He phoned Osborne and agreed rates only marginally cheaper than those originally mentioned. Osborne had already checked out flights; flying BA via Heathrow, he could get to Edinburgh shortly after noon the following day. Cammy arranged that Amy should meet him at Edinburgh Airport then. She had a number of friends who were happy to look after Sandy for a few hours and he had an early afternoon time in the medal. He was damned if he was going to miss it. He left the house, almost tasting the first pint.

Expecting an enthusiastic response, Amy accessed Cammy's account and showed her father Osborne's e-mail, explaining why they were hiring him. His reaction disappointed her. 'He certainly has a good opinion of himself,' he said, frowning. Exhausted by a taxing day, they slumped in front of the television before going early to bed.

3

'What's that?' Amy muttered, wakened by screeching cats in a neighbour's garden.

Smelling like a brewery, Cammy grunted and put his arm round her, affection she did not welcome. She lifted his hand and put it behind her. Feeling dampness, she woke fully. There was a smear of something wet on her hand. She switched on her bedside light and saw it was blood. Over the following days she would remember her spontaneous anger because she had changed the bed the previous morning. She tugged the sheet off Cammy, who sat up, looking indignant. She saw that the scar tissue over the knuckles of his right hand had broken and blood had seeped onto the clean sheet. There was a red stain on his t-shirt as well. Her hand felt sticky.

'What the hell have you been doing?' she hissed.

'What do you mean?' he slurred.

'You've been fighting, haven't you? And you're bleeding over everything.'

'Naw. Naw. I ... I grazed them on a wall.'

She didn't believe him but her priority was to stop the bleeding and get some more sleep. 'Well go and bandage it. No. I'll do it. I don't want blood all over the place. Come on.' She led him meekly to the bathroom where she applied a bandage tighter than strictly necessary. Then they returned to bed. Amy checked the time. It was eleven minutes past two. Ten minutes later, guttural snores sent her fuming to the spare room where sleep continued to elude her.

* * *

'McKellar? What is it?' Flick had nearly found sleep after a session with Verity, who was producing a set of teeth most crocodiles would be proud of. A call on her mobile was the last thing she wanted at two minutes to three.

'Sorry to disturb you, ma'am, but there's been a sudden death on The Scores here in St Andrews. Just in front of the castle. Sounds like it's a murder.' He sounded more genuinely apologetic than he would have a year and a half earlier.

Half-asleep, she struggled to put her brain into detective inspector mode. She knew she had to go to this one. 'Right, I'll be there in quarter of an hour. Can you come?'

'Yes, ma'am. I'll be there in five. There's a young PC from Cupar there now. He's out of his depth and phoned me as I live nearby. I told him to preserve the crime scene and note anyone who's there. I've called Dr Ralston to confirm death. I doubt if we'll be dealing with Lazarus.'

Flick ended the call. 'Sorry darling,' she said to her

husband, Fergus Maxwell, who was sitting up in bed looking sleepy and fed-up.

'I guess I can forget about the medal this morning,' he said, after she had explained. 'Don't worry. I'll be on Verity duty today.' He was also a detective inspector, though with the Dundee Division while Flick was with the Fife Division. He understood the imperatives of the job, imperatives that had wrecked many police marriages, not just in detective fiction. He understood, too, that Flick's career was at least as important to her as his was to him. Anxious that having a baby would set her back, a murder inquiry would give her an opportunity to show that she could successfully juggle police work and motherhood.

Pulling on her clothes, Flick felt her excitement mounting as the adrenaline began to flow. She had offered to get up as necessary for Verity during the Friday night to help Fergus in the New Golf Club medal that morning. Now he would have to cancel. She told herself she should feel sorrier than she did.

A sleek, confident-looking fox was the only living creature Flick saw on her drive through town. The far end of The Scores, the street nearest the North Sea leading from the Royal and Ancient to the ruined castle, was one-way. To get to the castle, and the body, Flick drove up North Street and down the narrow, cobbled North Castle Street. Near the end, a handful of lights burned in the windows of the quaint stone houses as spasms of electric blue splashed anachronistically over them. A police car blocked progress down The Scores. Beyond the car, two figures were moving about on the road opposite the castle. Flick's heartbeat was racing. She counted to five and stepped out of her car.

McKellar, in uniform and in his element, had taken charge. The young constable from Cupar, PC Dennis Austin, was tying white and blue incident tape round a tree. As Flick took in the scene, McKellar said, 'It looks awful like a murder, ma'am, and our victim is Mr Eric Cox, so there's going to be a right stushie. A witness says he saw Mr Cox struggling with someone then falling. That's the witness, in the back of the car. He says he's a witness anyway.' Flick made out a pale, scared-looking man peering out of a rear window. McKellar continued, 'Doc Ralston has confirmed death, he thinks by strangulation. He's just away. The ambulance too. We're now waiting for SOCOs from Dundee. Oh, I asked Dr MacGregor to come too. I thought you would want him to see the body ASAP. I told him you had asked me to call him. I hope you don't mind.'

Flick raised her eyebrows and went over to where the body lay. Cox was on his back, his torso on the road, one of his feet on the grass verge on the side opposite the castle, the other on the road. His hands seemed to be clawing at something round his neck and his tongue protruded rudely. There was blood coming from his nose. His head assumed an odd angle, his hair was a mess and his glasses were on the roadway beside him.

Flick took this in then nodded. 'Good. He makes the most of a visit to the crime scene.' Dr MacGregor was a showman. There were few murder trials in the East of Scotland which did not hear evidence from him, and very few juries which did not accept what he said.

'Oh fuck,' the young constable said, looking down.

'What's wrong?' Flick snapped.

'I think I've stood in some evidence, ma'am.'

'What do you mean?'

'Well according to the witness, the deceased was arguing with someone over a dog fouling the grass. And ...'

Ignoring McKellar's stifled laugh, Flick glared at Austin. 'Well don't make it any worse and don't move till the photographer's taken a shot of it and the SOCOs have a sample.' She turned to McKellar and, responding to his amusement, emitted a nervous giggle before saying, 'It's really not funny'.

Collecting herself, she looked down the dimly-lit Scores, imposing university buildings on both sides and, along the side opposite the castle, a grass verge and a wide pavement. To her right, the castle itself, battered to ruins by French guns centuries ago, had seen cruel torture and violent death, much of it inspired by religious beliefs. The body of a cardinal had been hung from the front wall whose irregular outline she could make out. Today's case meant a lot to her, but in the context of all that had happened here, it was nothing.

'Assuming for now he's only a witness, what does he have to say?' she asked McKellar, nodding towards the police car.

'He told Austin he was taking the air and heard an argument over a dog fouling the grass verge. It became heated and the two men started to struggle. One of them fell and our witness went back into his house. He lives in North Castle Street, ma'am. Twenty-five minutes later he thought he should check everything was all right and he found the body. He called 999. Austin and the ambulance were first here and when it looked like a murder, Austin phoned me at home.'

'Does he know the man he says Cox was fighting with?'

'He says no, but I've had dealings with him and it might be a good idea for me to have a proper word.'

'Well let's have one now. You lead.' She climbed into the front passenger seat and turned round while McKellar sat in the back. The little man shuffled as far away from him as possible. With thick, white hair brushed straight back and an unlined face, Flick reckoned he could be anything from forty to sixty-five. There was a smell of frying in the car, and she recognised the proprietor of one of the town's fish and chip shops.

'Hello, Dino,' McKellar said, a hint of surprise in his voice, 'What are you doing here at this time of night?'

'Oh Alex, it's awfy good tae see you.' The pale face lit up as he spoke. Flick had heard his voice on her few visits to his shop. It was distinctive – an Italian speaking English with a Scottish accent.

'It's not me you have to impress, Dino. This is Detective Inspector Fortune, and she wants the truth out of you now. Ma'am, this is Dino Rizzoli.'

Flick looked at him steadily and nodded.

He smiled at her then turned back to McKellar. 'I tell your boy there everything, Alex. It was busy night in the shop. The Lammas Market, you know. I go home and I need air so I go out for a wee while.' He shrugged his shoulders expressively. 'I hear men arguing. A dog had done poo-poo on grass but his owner didnae pick it up. The other man, he go, "You pick up or I call polis." He sound posh. The man with the dog say, "I havnae a bag for it," and they argue. Then the man with the dog, he punch posh man and posh man hits the floor. I go in. Stay out of road. Twenty-five minutes later, I go check he okay, but he dead and I call 999.'

McKellar said, 'So who was the man with the dog, Dino?'

'I couldnae make him out. Light no good.'

'Are you sure there was a man with a dog, Dino? There are some police who always suspect the person who finds the body, and I'm one of them.'

'No, Alex, no! You cannae think that about me!'

'And if we think you've been hiding things from us, you might find the food hygene people coming round to inspect your chip shop. Now describe the dog.'

Dino stared out of the window then said quietly, 'It was Cammy Smith's dog. Looks daft. Doon at the front, up at the back. Everyone knows it. Benjy. But Cammy, he is good man. I no want to see him in trouble.'

'And you did recognise Cammy? He punched the man?'

'Yes.' Dino nodded miserably.

'Did he do anything else to him?'

'Not that I see. When posh man hit the floor, I go. I dinnae want involved.'

'Well I'm afraid you are, whether you want to be or not. I'll have to take a statement from you before you go,' McKellar said sternly.

Flick told Dino to wait and got out of the car, gesturing McKellar to follow. As she shut the door she heard the little man say something about paying for chips in future.

'Who is Cammy Smith?' she asked.

McKellar pulled a face. 'He's a local plumber. Good business ...'

'Smith Plumbers? We've used them a couple of times.'

'But ma'am, he's the murderer Waldron's son-in-law. Cox was demonstrating outside his house yesterday.'

'Oh, that's interesting. We'd better ...' she was cut off by a car with a flashing blue light driving the wrong way up The Scores. A second car followed. First out was the photographer. His cameras, video and still, were soon busy. It took little time for the scene of crime examination routine to kick in; more tape, sterile suits, a tent over the body. There was quiet banter at Austin's expense as his foot was photographed and samples taken. Meanwhile McKellar took Dino's statement and got him to sign it.

'Good morning, Detective Inspector!' the plummy voice was behind her. Dr MacGregor, the pathologist had arrived. He burbled on, 'If it is now morning, that is. You seem to specialise in exotically murdered corpses. What a grand place to choose! I hope this one is worth losing beauty sleep over.'

'Thank you for coming, Doctor. This could be high-profile.' She explained about Cox.

'Well thank you for authorising a taxi. I dined well last night, and quite wisely, but perhaps not wisely enough for the new drink-driving limit.'

'Better safe than sorry,' she said and looked at McKellar, still in the police car with Dino. Some bean-counter would be bound to quibble over the taxi. He had been right to authorise it, but had done a lot in her name without her knowledge.

'My thoughts exactly,' the doctor said. He slipped on a sterile suit and disappeared into the tent, now glowing like a light bulb.

Fifteen minutes later he emerged. 'He's been dead between one and two hours. Definitely murder. By strangulation, using his own bow tie. One of the few advantages of these dreadful clip-on bow ties is that they are less easily turned into lethal weapons. He had one you tie yourself.'

'Was much force required?' Flick asked.

'It would depend on how much resistance the deceased put up. He had a bleeding nose, looked as if he had been punched. If he cracked his head when he went down he might not have offered much of a fight, although he did put his hands to his neck in an attempt to defend himself. I'll be able to give you more after the post mortem.'

'Thank you, Doctor. You have been most helpful as usual.'

'And I have yet to tell you the strangest thing about this corpse. I have reason to think he may have been playing golf shortly before his death.'

'Golf? Shortly?'

'Within a few hours. I shall explain. I found many grains of sand in his hair and ears. It appears to be the sort of sand used for bunkers on the golf course. And there were more on the left side of his head than the right side. I don't know if you are a golfer, but I know your husband plays. When you are hitting your ball out of a bunker you disturb a good deal of sand, which flies up and generally in the direction of your shot. Some goes straight up and settles on you. As a right-handed player has his left side facing the hole, most sand hitting his head will hit the left side. There was a significant quantity of what I think is bunker sand adhering to the left side of Mr Cox's rather greasy hair. And in his left ear. I would have been surprised if anyone had gone out for the evening without washing it out. So I deduce that he may have been playing golf when most people were in bed and he should have been. As usual, I am trying to give you an early steer and all this may change after the post mortem and examination of samples.'

'That's extraordinary. Thank you, Doctor. When's the post mortem?'

'Not till Monday. Now, I plan to try to get a couple of hours' sleep before the medal at Barry this afternoon. Good hunting, Detective Inspector.'

Flick thanked him again then turned to the crime scene investigators who had found no wallet, credit cards or mobile phone. Flick ordered a search of the general area in daylight and authorised the removal of the body.

'Now we should pay Mr Cammy Smith a visit,' she said.

McKellar said, 'Dino's right, ma'am. Smith is a good man. I can see him thumping Cox, but not strangling him.'

'We have to follow the evidence, Alex,' Flick replied.

* * *

The dawn chorus had started and the first light of the new day was creeping over St Andrews when Flick pressed the Smiths' front door bell, giving a long, hard ring. Surprisingly quickly a cross-looking woman in a nighty answered. It took Flick a moment to recognise her as one of the mums at Verity's nursery.

'Mrs Smith, sorry to bother you,' she said, feeling

awkward. She introduced herself, McKellar and the other two uniformed constables with her. Surprised then alarmed, Amy let them in. By the time Flick had told her that they needed to see Cammy in connection with a murder she was aghast.

'He's upstairs, asleep,' she said, her voice shaky. 'I'll go up and waken him.'

'I'm afraid we must come with you,' Flick said. As they climbed the stairs, Benjy emerged from the kitchen, growling and baring his teeth. His unusual appearance gave him a wild, unpredictable look.

Cammy was lying on his back, mouth open, snoring loudly. Amy shook him awake. 'It's the police to see you,' she hissed, wanting to ask him what he had done, but afraid to do so.

'Cameron Smith, I am detaining you under the Criminal Justice Act in respect of the murder of Eric Cox ...' The rest of Flick's set speech was drowned out by a wail from Amy.

'What?' Cammy sat on the edge of the bed, rubbing his eyes.

Leaving McKellar and a male constable with him while he dressed, Flick went downstairs with Amy and the other constable. They met Benjy at the foot.

Flick, who was not a dog-lover, knew not to show fear. Observing the thick hair round the dog's bottom, she nodded at the PC and asked Amy if they might take a sample of the dog's hair and a smear from his rectum. 'Why?' Amy asked wearily.

'To preserve possible scientific evidence, Mrs

Smith,' Flick said. 'If you say no we'll be back with a warrant in a couple of hours.'

'All right.' She sounded as defeated as she felt.

Flick called Austin, who had been stationed in the garden backing on to the Smiths' in case Cammy had done a runner.

'You hold the dog,' Flick told Austin, but his attempts to hold the struggling, snarling animal were laughable. Flick looked to Mrs Smith for assistance, but her face was set; Amy was damned if she was going to help them convict her husband.

'Go to the kitchen and get scissors,' Flick commanded the second PC.

He returned with a pair of scissors and stood irresolutely, watching Austin make tentative moves at Benjy's head, only to pull back from the snapping jaws.

Flick told herself it was time to show leadership. She had seen how a vet subdues a difficult dog and knew speed was of the essence. In a single move she put Benjy's head in a secure headlock and got down beside him, his jaws out of harm's way. The second PC used the borrowed scissors to cut locks of matted hair from the dog's rear and stuck a cotton bud into his rectum. Austin bagged the samples. Satisfied, Flick released Benjy, standing back rapidly. This was unnecessary as, tail between his long back legs, the dog fled to the kitchen.

It was not long before Cammy came down, looking terrified. Behind him, McKellar grasped a number of polythene bags containing the clothes he had discarded hours earlier. Amy threw her arms round his neck then Cammy was led by McKellar to the waiting police car, one of the PCs escorting them.

As they went out the front door they heard a child's voice shouting, 'Where Dadda, where Dadda?'

4

Leaving McKellar in charge in St Andrews with instructions to search the Smiths' house for the dead man's possessions, Flick went in the car with Cammy to Cupar. The formalities of detention were completed and a grumpy police surgeon examined him, in particular the injury to his right knuckle. He said he did not want a solicitor. Before he could change his mind, Flick decided to interview him on tape, PC Austin with her.

'Were you on The Scores late at night?' she asked after cautioning him.

'Yes.'

'Did you see Mr Eric Cox?'

'If that's the boy's name.'

Flick raised an eyebrow. 'So you met someone?'

'What if I did?'

'Did you have a dog with you?'

'Yes.'

'Did you have an argument with a man about a dog?'

He shifted in his chair. 'What if I did?'

'Are you saying you did?'

He glared at her. 'Well, yes.'

'And did you not recognise the man? He was on the Scottish News yesterday demonstrating outside your house.'

Cammy stared at the scruffy wooden table in front of him, as if it might somehow inspire his swimming brain but he could think of nothing to say.

'Mr Smith, a witness says you argued with Mr Cox because he objected to your dog fouling the verge and you didn't pick it up. Is that true?'

For a moment Cammy fidgeted, his eyes avoiding Flick's, then he said, 'I'd been out for a few pints and that, and I was pissed when I got home. Benjy wanted out so I took him a walk. He crapped near the castle and this boy started on at me for not picking it up, but I didn't have anything with me. He was right arrogant, the boy, and I punched him once. He went down but I can't have killed him surely?'

'Did you not recognise him?'

He shook his head in frustration. 'Well, yes I did. He was arrogant, as I said, and he had no right to cause a disturbance outside my house.'

'Did you do anything to his neck?'

He looked puzzled then scared. 'His neck? No, I caught him on his nose.'

'Are you sure?'

'Yes.' He sounded indignant.

'Did you not strangle him as he lay on the ground?'

'Christ. No. I went straight home.'

Flick noted panic in his voice. 'Did you not use

his bow tie to throttle him?' She spoke softly, with understanding, inviting him to confide in her.

'No, I say.'

'Do you not remember his bow tie?'

He wrinkled his face. 'He had something like a tie loose round his neck.'

'Handy for strangling him?'

'Naw, naw, naw.' He was shouting now.

'Mr Cox was punched and strangled. You admit you punched him. If you didn't strangle him, who did?'

'Not me. I've had enough of this. I want to go home.' He got up, scraping his chair noisily.

'Sit down, Mr Smith,' Flick said, firmly but unemotionally, as Austin half-rose, ready to tackle him. 'You're still detained and more needs to be done before the next step.'

Breathing deeply, he sat down. 'I want a lawyer,' he said.

He was entitled to one. Flick terminated the interview.

* * *

Some time after seven, Flick thought she should call the duty fiscal. The sharp voice of Harriet Cowan came down the line and Flick's heart sank. She was the most awkward of the local fiscals, and she seemed to get a kick out of criticising the police, adopting an air of intellectual superiority Flick hated.

'Why didn't you call me sooner?' she demanded.

'Because there was nothing for you to do at the crime scene and I've heard too many crown lawyers moaning about being dragged from their beds for no good reason.'

'This is a high-profile murder. I should have been called immediately.'

Flick knew she had a point but was not going to apologise. 'I made sure that everything that had to be done was done. And I'm calling you now.'

'Well I'm not happy. What evidence have you got?'

Evidence that your nickname of 'Harridan Harriet' is well justified, Flick felt like saying. Instead she told her all that she knew.

'Charge him.'

'Smith?'

'Of course.'

'Are you sure we have enough evidence?'

'Yes, plenty. Remember, I'm the lawyer. He can appear in court on Monday. Is he fit to be detained?'

'Yes. He's seen the doctor.'

'Well at least you've done something right.'

'I'm not sure he's guilty. I felt, from his reactions, he was telling the truth in his interview. I can't help feeling there may be more to this than meets the eye. What about the sand in the victim's hair? Why no mobile or wallet or credit cards? Should we not try to learn more before we charge someone?'

'I hope I made myself clear, Detective Inspector. Charge him "that you did punch him and strangle him and did murder him." And do it now. I'll see you on Monday.' The phone clicked.

Flick shook her head then, with the duty solicitor present and Austen standing wide-eyed beside her, she placed Cammy under arrest and charged him with the murder of Eric Cox. Aghast, he replied, 'I didn't kill him.'

5

'We keep on telling people not to drive when they're tired so I thought I should get you to take me through,' Flick told DC Billy Di Falco as they set off for Edinburgh, where Cox's mother lived. She was his only next of kin. 'But actually I want to see what you think of this one.'

She was describing the scene when her mobile rang. It was McKellar. The search of the Smiths' house had proved fruitless but a journalist and a photographer had turned up there. 'Already?' she asked.

'Yes ma'am. And they seem to know what's been going on. They've been asking about Cammy Smith and Cox too. I've kept them outside for now.'

'Tell them a body has been found and that a person has been detained. There will be nothing further until the next of kin have been informed. And try to find out who leaked this.'

Turning to Di Falco, Flick said, 'There's something very odd about this case. I want to break the news to Cox's mother myself and find out as much as I can about him. I'm sorry, as it's not going to be pleasant.'

'Have you contacted HQ ma'am? They might

think this is a job for their new mobile unit for serious crime.'

'No. Like most of us, I don't like Police Scotland with their mania for over-centralisation. I'm going to keep this for us as long as I can. After all, we have made an arrest so we can say there's nothing for them to do.'

An hour and a quarter later they parked in a leafy street in South Edinburgh outside a substantial semi-detached stone house with a neat front garden. Flick double-checked the address. 'Here we go,' she said.

The lady who answered the bell appeared to have been up for hours. On the stout side, she was immaculate from her carefully waved white hair to her neat black shoes. 'Yes?' she said, her tone imperious. She agreed that she was Mrs Rosaleen Cox. When Flick explained that they needed to come in to talk to her, she took great care inspecting their warrants before stepping aside. 'A woman on her own has to be so careful these days. Some of us warned long ago that law and order would break down and, sure enough, it has.' She glared at Flick, daring her to contradict her.

Seated in the comfortable, tasteful sitting room, Flick noted the collection of oil paintings, antique furniture and valuable-looking rugs, some no doubt inherited, others accumulated over the years. In pride of place on the marquetry table at the bay window, beside a vase containing fresh dahlias, was a faded colour photograph. It showed Mrs Cox in thinner days, wearing a formal, blue dress and a large hat. She was posing stiffly beside a man with an upright bearing and a superior expression, wearing morning dress. His hand rested on the shoulder of a teenage boy Flick recognised as Eric, also in morning dress. Behind them, Buckingham Palace loomed grandly and unmistakably. They must have thought it too common to display whatever medal might have been awarded, Flick thought, and had it been a knighthood, this lady would unquestionably have called herself Lady Cox. She immediately reprimanded herself. Tiredness was making her chippy. Apart from a graduation photograph of Eric and a grainy black and white wedding photograph, there was no other portrayal of the family. Eric was probably her only surviving close relative. From her haughty expression, she had no inkling of the devastating news she was about to hear. Flick braced herself mentally before shattering the comfortable bubble in which this unlikeable yet somehow pathetic woman lived.

Disbelief then anger flitted across her face before she crumpled into a howling ball of grief, rocking to and fro on her elegant cream sofa. Another mother stricken by the loss of a child. Flick suddenly thought of Verity and felt herself shudder.

'How did he die? What happened?' Mrs Cox cried.

Flick gave her the essential details, including Smith's arrest, then waited for some minutes, wondering whether she should put her arm round the heaving shoulders and deciding that this lady might not appreciate it. 'Is there anyone we could call?' she asked.

'Jenny Middlemiss, across the road,' she blurted between sobs.

Di Falco found this friend in. An unfussy, practical person, she managed to calm Mrs Cox, explaining that the police needed to ask her some questions. Flick assured her that there was no hurry.

Bred to keep a stiff upper lip, Mrs Cox composed herself sufficiently to declare that, no doubt at Waldron's instigation, Smith had clearly laid a trap for Eric. She proudly told them of his successful schooldays at the prestigious Edinburgh Academy, his law degree and his days as an advocate. 'But the bar's not what it used to be,' she said, sniffing back tears. 'Eric was too interested in the just result. Everyone else was out to win. It wasn't for him. So he went into politics full-time. He knew the Conservatives were struggling in Scotland, so he focused on the scandal of criminals getting out of jail long before they should. He was making a name for himself, really achieving something.' He wasn't married, she explained; 'hadn't found the right girl yet' and had been living off the income from the trust his grandfather had set up.

Reluctantly, Mrs Cox permitted the officers to search his room and remove his computer. The computer was an ordinary laptop. In one drawer they found papers relating to a number of cases. Cox had been nothing if not thorough and had gathered materials relating to the original crimes. At the top of the pile were print-outs of archive reports relating to Spencer's murder and Waldron's trial. Di Falco collected them all for examination at the police office.

On their way out, Flick asked if Eric had used a mobile phone.

'Oh yes,' his mother replied. 'He had what he called an i-phone and used it a lot. In fact he phoned me yesterday evening saying he'd be staying in St Andrews as he was going to have dinner with some old friends of that murderer Waldron. I couldn't understand why. I'd been expecting him back here. It was the last time I spoke to him.' She sniffed loudly.

'Did he say who these friends of Waldron's were or where they ate?' Flick asked.

'No, he was on the phone for only a minute.' She dissolved into tears once more. After getting the mobile number, the officers left the room quietly.

'It was justice that he wanted,' his mother wailed after them. 'Justice was everything to him.'

Once back in the car Flick asked, 'Well, what do you make of it?'

'I don't know ma'am,' Di Falco said. 'A surprising suspect and an odd victim.'

'Indeed. And I know someone who will find this interesting. He doesn't live far from here and it's time for coffee.'

* * *

'I am sorry Melanie is out seeing a friend,' Bagawath Chandavarkar said as he set down a tray of Willow Pattern mugs and a cafetiere. 'She has left me to swot for my inspector's exam.' He nodded at the books and folders scattered round the chair where he had been sitting. 'It's Java,' he added as he started to pour.

'Better than what you used to make in Wimbledon CID?' Flick asked, looking round the comfortable sitting room with a high ceiling, a neat cornice and a variety of interesting and colourful paintings. Known as Baggo, he had wangled a move from the Serious Fraud Office in London to the equivalent unit in Edinburgh so that he might live with Melanie Arbuthnot, an advocate at the Scottish bar whom he had met during an investigation into a murder in the law courts.

'Much better than the Wimbledon muck, Flick.' He turned down the volume of the CD he was playing. Flick thought she recognised *Turandot*.

'So Baggo, how's the great romance going?' she asked.

His hand jerked and a splash of coffee landed on the table. Flick had taken him by surprise, not, as she supposed, with her question about his love life, but with her easy use of 'Baggo'. Her excessive formality really was becoming a thing of the past. Carefully, he wiped the coffee before replying.

'We are very happy right now. We have been living together for nearly six months, since I got my move to Edinburgh. This splendid flat is Melanie's. Both sets of parents are making veiled inquiries about the future. Melanie's are very polite but I sense that they are not enamoured of the prospect of their lovely daughter marrying a wog, even a nice wog like me.'

'I wish you wouldn't use that word,' Flick snapped.

Baggo grinned. He could still wind her up. 'Oh, I'm entitled as I am one. My parents are far worse. They still want me to marry a nice Brahmin girl. They regard Melanie as being about as undesirable a wife for me as an untouchable. It is not easy for us as we both love our parents despite their prejudices, but who said life was supposed to be a piece of cake? Talking of which, how is it to be back from maternity leave?'

'Wearing. Particularly when Verity's teething. Tiredness can become part of your way of life.'

'What about you, Billy?' Baggo asked. 'Are you still playing the field?'

Di Falco flashed his film star grin. 'Yes, and if settling down means what you two are going through, I plan to keep playing.'

The influence of his boyhood in Mumbai coming across strongly in his voice, Baggo said, 'You are a most wise man. But to what do I owe this pleasure? Are you just wandering round Morningside looking for free coffee?'

Flick had always been irritated by his caricature Indian act, which most people found funny. 'We've been breaking the bad news to a next of kin,' she said sharply.

He frowned. 'You need a DI and a DC to do that?'

Flick nodded. 'That strange man Eric Cox was found dead in St Andrews last night, you know the "life should mean life" campaigner. He was strangled. We've arrested a man, Smith, who is the son-in-law of that murderer Waldron, you know the one released because he's dying of cancer? Waldron is staying with Smith and his wife. Yesterday Cox demonstrated outside Smith's house. There was an item about it on the Scottish News last night. It seems there was a late-night confrontation between Smith and Cox over Smith's dog fouling a verge. I interviewed him and Smith seemed reluctantly honest when he admitted punching Cox, but adamant when he denied strangling him. There's a bit of me inclined to believe him, though there's no other suspect. Cox's next of kin was his mother, who lives just up the road from here. The fiscal insisted I should charge Smith with murder but I wanted to learn as much as I could about the victim, so here we are.'

'What did you learn?'

She turned to Di Falco. 'What do you think, Billy, apart from the fact that he was a bit strange?'

'Cox was a mummy's boy. Very traditional. In the best and the worst senses. Ambitious, clever. Liked showing off. Believed in law and order, hankering after a golden age that didn't really exist. Maybe a closet gay. He could never tell his mother if he was. She is normally a force of nature. He probably had no real friends. Was out of tune with the rest of society. That's my guess. It's odd that he should have met some of Waldron's friends for dinner instead of returning to Edinburgh.'

Flick asked, 'And why were his i-phone and wallet missing? Why had he been playing golf in the dark, if MacGregor is right?'

'Playing golf in the dark?' Baggo asked.

'Yes. MacGregor found bunker sand in his hair,' Flick said.

Baggo grinned. 'It is not unknown for quite respectable people to take advantage of the short Northern nights and play a few illicit holes at this time of year.' Again he hammed up the Indian accent, never able to resist tweaking Flick's tail. 'This is normally done after a good deal of liquid refreshment. Only recently, I myself …'

'Never mind,' Flick said quickly.

'I scored surprisingly well,' Baggo said, undeterred. 'But I think you have a cracker here. I just wish there was a financial element for me to get my teeth into.'

They worked well together, Baggo's willingness to bend the rules stopping short of what Flick regarded as indefensible. He added flair to her ability to evaluate and make deductions from evidence. She said, 'Well I think it's quite complex enough already. But if we find evidence of fraud we'll be on the phone. Come on, Billy. We'd best be off.'

They thanked Baggo for the coffee and wished him good luck in his exam. With Flick dozing in the front seat, Di Falco drove back to Cupar.

6

'So murder is the family business, then?' ex-Detective Inspector Noel Osborne asked as he lit up a cigarette and blew the smoke towards Amy, who was concentrating on taking the correct lane as she drove out of Edinburgh Airport.

'Both my father and my husband are innocent. That's why you're here,' she replied through gritted teeth.

He chuckled. 'That's what they all say, Doll.'

It had been a terrible day for her and it was getting worse. Panic-stricken after Cammy's arrest, she had, in desperation, phoned her step-father, who had promised to do what he could. But he had little experience of criminal law and required to mug up. When he had arrived at Cupar police office, a bulky, loose-leaf book on criminal procedure under his arm, he was told that the duty solicitor had already advised Mr Smith, who had been charged with murder and was being kept in custody at least until court on Monday. Sounding genuinely sorry, H-man had phoned Amy to report.

When, holding back tears, she told her father what had happened, he looked sadly at her. 'I'm sorry if I've brought this on you,' was all that he said then went to his room, slamming the door.

Little Sandy had sensed that something was wrong and kept looking for his daddy. Amy could not stop herself from imagining what it would be like to bring him up as she had been, with a convicted murderer for a father. It was a prospect that terrified her.

Leaving the little boy with her friend, Maggie, she had gone to pick up Osborne. On her way she had called in at Cupar, where she had been allowed a brief meeting with Cammy. He had told her what he had told the police, swearing it was true, and she believed him; she could see him, drunk, walloping a man like Cox, but she could not imagine him strangling him as he lay on the ground. He had insisted that she should phone the golf club to cancel his time in the medal; she wondered if he realised quite how serious his situation was.

And now she had her white knight, Osborne. But he was not what she had hoped for. Entering the terminal, he had looked grumpy and dishevelled and smelled of drink. He had lit up as soon as he was outside; this was his second cigarette since landing. Worst of all, he seemed to find Cammy's arrest amusing in some twisted way. It was time she put him right.

Stopping the car abruptly and ignoring the horns that sounded behind her, she turned to her passenger. 'Look, Mr Osborne, I am prepared to pay you good money, but only if you do your job. That is to prove my husband and my father innocent. No more, no less. And unless you are willing to start off on the assumption that they are both innocent, I will turn this car round and dump you and your scabby suitcase back at that terminal. Without a penny. Do I make myself clear?'

Osborne was taken aback. He wasn't used to women talking to him like that. But this one meant business. 'Keep your hair on, Doll. It was only a joke.'

'Well it's my family so I don't find it funny. And never call me Doll again. Do we understand each other?'

He attempted a half smile. 'Yes, Do... Mrs er ...'

'Smith. Shouldn't be too hard to remember. Unless you're drunk, of course.'

She looked at him steadily, seriously considering her options. But, objectionable or not, half-hearted or not, he was the only person on her team. Sounding as positive as possible, she said, 'It'll be an hour anyway till we're back in St Andrews. You may want to sleep during the journey.'

* * *

'Ouch!' Billy Di Falco exclaimed as the Passat that had accelerated past them on the dual carriageway near the end of the 50 mph limit leaving Glenrothes was flashed by a speed camera van. 'That's a sneaky place to speed-trap. They must need to boost their statistics.'

'Did we get caught?' Flick asked. She had been

half-dozing, half-thinking in the front passenger seat. Had she been awake and looking round she would not have liked what she saw: lolling in the passenger seat of the speeding Passat, his mouth open, was her old boss from Wimbledon days, and nemesis, ex-Inspector No.

'No, ma'am, it was that car ahead,' Di Falco said.

'Why should Cox change his plans and go to dinner with friends of Waldron's?' Flick asked. This had been bothering her in her semi-awake state.

'That's what I've been wondering, ma'am. It sounds as if it was an odd evening, with night golf thrown in.'

'When we get back, would you try to find out where they ate, and, more important, who they were? I think that's the obvious starting-point.'

'I agree ma'am. When we get back I'll make inquiries round the local eating places.'

'Good.' Flick closed her eyes and tried to empty her head. Even ten minutes' sleep would help.

* * *

'So you're here to prove my innocence?' Peter Waldron asked Osborne, his voice and face full of doubt. When Amy told her father that the private detective had arrived, he had wheeled himself through to the downstairs sitting room.

Desensitised though he was by many years of negative reactions, Osborne realised he was not making a good impression. The woman, Mrs Smith was stroppy and he didn't want to tangle with her. When they entered her home, which seemed too posh to lead right onto the street, a crazy-looking mongrel had growled ferociously and a small brat had burst into tears. Now this grey-haired old lag on his last legs was giving him the sort of sniffy once-over he had been used to getting from senior officers during his time in the force.

'I'm a detective, not a bleeding miracle-worker.' He spoke defiantly, forcefully. He wasn't going to let these people push him around.

'I never imagined you were,' Waldron countered smoothly. 'As you may know, I don't have long to live, so let's get started.' He turned his wheelchair smartly and left the room. Osborne heaved himself out of the low sofa and followed him into an empty corridor.

'Here!' Osborne entered the room from which the voice had come. It was full of paper, arranged in neat piles on the bed and on the dressing table. Osborne's jaw dropped; surely he was not expected to wade his way through all this crap? 'Shut the door,' Waldron snapped.

Osborne did so slowly and turned to face his new client. 'As I said, I'm a detective and a fucking good one. You'd better believe it. I work on instinct and gut reaction learned the hard way. Now, what's the story?' He took out his cigarettes.

'Please don't smoke here.'

The two men eyeballed each other. Osborne was the one to give in, but not gracefully. 'I suppose you like your room to smell of jail,' he said, replacing the packet in his pocket. 'So, as I said, what's the story?'

Waldron ignored the insult. 'It's all here.' Gesturing towards a pile of bound volumes with typing on the front, 'These are the parts of the evidence at the trial that were extended for the Appeal Court ...'

'Give me the short version, and start from the beginning.'

Waldron stared at him, his dark, intense eyes making Osborne think of rabbit turds in porridge. Was he going to refuse to speak to him? That would be a bummer; Osborne needed the money.

'I'm here to help you.'

Another pause.

'In 1984 I was convicted of murdering Tony Spencer. Someone, not me, scratched his arm with a broken golf tee coated with poison as the Open Championship reached its climax here at St Andrews. The tee was later found in my jacket pocket, wrapped in a bit of newspaper. It was planted. The poison came from the skin of a South American frog. I kept a number of these frogs at my home. I had a collection of rare reptiles. Spencer had been having an affair with my wife. I was supposed to have said to a detective sergeant: "The bastard was asking for it. He'd been shagging my wife." I didn't say that. The detective sergeant verballed me.' He paused. 'You'll have verballed people yourself, I assume?'

Osborne felt his face twitching. He found this seriously ill man who smelled of jail strangely intimidating. 'A few,' he admitted, 'but only if I knew they were guilty.'

'That's what they all say, I bet. Anyway that was the case against me and the jury found me guilty. On the day of the murder my wife and I had been guests of a property company at lunch. There was a group of us. We called ourselves "The Jolly Boys". We met up to have fun, generally with a lot of drink, and we helped each other in business if we could. For reasons I'll explain, it must have been one of them, or their wives, who killed Spencer and framed me. Don't you want to take notes?'

Osborne stopped scratching his crotch and felt in his jacket pockets. He found the e-ticket for his flight and a biro. There was a wooden chair which he moved beside the table and sat down. 'The Jolly Boys,' he repeated and wrote on the back of the ticket.

'Yes. There were six of us. The original group of five was formed at Edinburgh University. We were all law students. The unofficial leader was Jocelyn Montpellier, known as Joss. There was Tony Spencer, Jimmy Lightbody and Kevin McPhail, whom we nicknamed "the kid". We all came to work in the East Neuk of Fife, Montpellier, Spencer, Lightbody and I as solicitors, McPhail as the manager of East Neuk Properties Ltd, the company he set up. We invited Hugh Harkins, who was a year younger than me but in the same firm, to join us. Montpellier's wife was called Georgia, Spencer's Mary, Lightbody's Norma and McPhail's Hannah. I don't know what the present situation is. I was married to Susan. Harkins was single but married Susan after I was convicted and she had divorced me. Anyway it was the eleven of us who lunched together courtesy of Kevin McPhail's company on the last day of the Open. We all had a lot to drink.' He paused to allow Osborne to finish writing.

'Okay, you say you were framed …'

'I was framed.'

'Okay, okay. But how did the real killer get the poison?'

'Susan and I had held a lunch party the previous Sunday. The same people as were at the lunch on the last day of the Open. Someone must have reached into the glass tank and removed one of the frogs. I had nine at the time and there were plenty of places in the tank for them to hide, so you seldom could see all nine at once. I was very proud of my collection. Susan used to say I bored people going on about it. I showed anyone who seemed interested.'

'So one of them must have planned the murder. Why?'

'I don't know. Spencer never really grew up. He was a womaniser and a heavy drinker, but I can't see why any of the rest of us should want to kill him.'

'Apart from you, if he was shagging your wife.'

Waldron glared but continued, 'I suppose Mary Spencer might have had enough, but she'd have got a good settlement on divorce.'

'So how exactly was he killed?'

'After lunch we stayed in the hospitality tent and watched the golf on television and had a few more drinks. Then, as the leaders turned for home, we all went to the mound behind the seventeenth green. We could see what was happening on both of the last two holes. We stayed more or less together but we all moved around, jostling so we could get a better view. It must have happened when the championship became really exciting. Spencer collapsed as Tom Watson was playing the eighteenth. The poison was quick-acting, so the scratch on his arm must have been inflicted minutes before, just about as Seve holed the winning putt on the eighteenth. At first everyone thought it was some sort of fit, but the post mortem revealed that he had been poisoned. Because I had my collection, and because of Spencer's affair with Susan, attention was focused on me. They searched my house and found the broken tee coated in poison and wrapped in newspaper in the right pocket of the jacket I'd worn on the day. I've no idea who put it there.' He pointed a shaky finger at Osborne. 'If I'd done it, I'd have dropped the tee on the ground to be trampled by the crowd. It would never have been found.'

'Do you say the killer must have slipped it into your pocket after he – or she – had used it on Spencer?'

'That must have been what happened. We were all shocked and we hung around for a bit, speaking to the police, comforting Mary. I took Susan home. We lived in Hepburn Gardens, not far away, and we walked. It was awkward between us, for obvious reasons. She was upset, but hiding it.' He grimaced but kept his voice steady.

'Do you think the killer wanted both you and Spencer out of the way, him dead and you in jail?'

'I do.'

'What if whoever did the post mortem didn't find the poison and signed it off as death due to natural causes?'

'I've asked myself that. Perhaps the killer would have planted ideas in Mary's head so she'd ask for a second opinion.'

'Tell me about the verbal.'

'It was the Wednesday after Spencer's death. Susan and I were at home, having dinner. The police came with a search warrant. I was taken by surprise and Susan was too. I identified the clothes I'd worn at the Open and they found the tee in the right hand pocket of the jacket. It was no doubt the newspaper wrapping that drew their attention to it. After the pathologist had identified the poison they must have learned about my collection and about Susan's affair with Spencer. It was an older man, Detective Sergeant Thomson, who found the tee and arrested me then and there. I'm supposed to have made the damaging remark in the car on the way to Cupar police station. There was a young constable in uniform sitting beside me in the back seat and he corroborated Thomson's evidence.'

'And what did you say, or they said you said?'

Osborne corrected himself but earned a glare from his client.

'"The bastard was asking for it. He'd been shagging my wife." I was a solicitor and I'm not stupid enough to have said anything like that.'

'Hmm.' Osborne took a careful note, playing for time to think. His hand drifted towards his crotch, he scratched then stopped himself. This was the first time he had been engaged to prove someone's innocence and he didn't like it. If it hadn't been for the money he'd happily walk away. He found the talk about verbals particularly unsettling. During his time in the Met he'd been regarded as a master of the art, and Thomson had done well with this one. No one would believe Waldron would have said "It's a fair cop, gov," or anything like that. This verbal showed the suspect's strong dislike of the deceased, proved he had a motive, and would lose sympathy from the jury. A cracker. Osborne himself could not have done better. And a verbal had been needed; the rest of the evidence was circumstantial, and if the witnesses had clammed up about the affair and the jury didn't hear about it, another man the police knew to be guilty might have walked free. He'd have done the same himself. But he was not going to tell Waldron that. 'Thomson was an older man?' he asked.

'He was fifty-two at the trial.'

'So eighty-three now?'

'Or dead.'

'And the younger one who corroborated him?'

'His name was McKellar. Twenty-one at the trial, so fifty-two now. I remember being shocked at how someone so young could tell lies on oath so shamelessly.'

A promising copper, Osborne thought. 'Do you know what became of him?' he asked.

'No. Have you any more questions before I run through these materials?' He waved towards the piles of paper. He was slumped in his wheelchair, tired by the exchange.

'Not at the moment.'

Waldron wheeled himself to the bed and pointed to each pile in turn. 'This is the judge's charge to the jury. These are the notes of the bits of the evidence the Appeal Court ordered to be extended. This is the Appeal Court decision. These are my notes about the evidence and the witnesses. This is my correspondence with the Scottish Criminal Case Review Board. This is my correspondence with my MP. This is my correspondence with my solicitors. You'll see I sacked the first lot after the appeal and engaged a second firm. They still act for me. Lastly, these are the papers relating to my parole hearings. You'll want to take them away and read them now so you can start tomorrow.'

'And what, exactly, am I supposed to do after all this time?'

'Go round, make a nuisance of yourself, rattle some cages.' He smiled. 'I bet you're good at that.'

For the first time, Osborne felt a liking for his client. Rattling cages was something he enjoyed and he had too few opportunities in retirement. He bundled the papers into the polythene bags lying at the end of the bed. He had no intention of wasting an evening wading through them, but over the next few days he would certainly make a nuisance of himself.

'My daughter will give you the contact details you need. If you need to speak to me, ring the house phone.'

'You don't have a mobile?'

'Not worthwhile getting one.'

Disconcerted, Osborne grinned nervously. 'I suppose not. But remember how long Megrahi lasted after pulling the same trick as you.' He turned to leave.

'I'll want daily up-dates. And shut the door.'

In the hall Osborne found Amy, who handed him a piece of paper with names, addresses and phone numbers. He shoved it into a jacket pocket.

'I'll take you to your digs,' she said.

'But I wanted a hotel,' Osborne complained as the car stopped outside a guest house in Murray Park, which led off North Street.

'They were all booked up,' Amy lied. 'It is the tourist season, you know. Janis Gillespie will look after you very well,' she added. And keep an eye on you she thought to herself; she knew Janis well.

With bad grace, Osborne scrambled out of the car and hefted his case and the bags of documents into the B and B.

'Don't let him down,' Amy shouted at his back before driving away.

7

'Yes, the JBs were at their usual table last night,' Julie
Lewis told Billy Di Falco. 'You'd be best speaking to
Amanda as she served them.' Julie was the owner
of The Adamson, a bistro-style restaurant in South
Street which, after a few phone calls, Di Falco had
identified as the place where Cox had eaten. Julie had
seen the item about St Andrews on the early evening
news and recognised Cox later when he arrived at the
restaurant; he had been with diners she knew well.

It was the end of the lunch service. Di Falco had
been shown to a quiet table near the back and given a
coffee. 'He was with the JBs?' he asked. 'Who are they?'

'That's what they call themselves. Short for "Jolly
Boys". A group who meet for dinner every month or
so.'

'What can you tell me about them?'

Julie shrugged and pushed her blonde hair back
from her face. 'They're very respectable, solicitors
mostly.'

Di Falco could see she was uneasy talking to
the police about good customers. He gave her what
colleagues called his 'Hollywood treatment'. 'It is a
murder inquiry,' he said gently.

Responding more to the toothpaste commercial smile than the admonition she said, 'There's four of them. Sometimes it's just them and sometimes their wives join them. Last night the booking was for eight covers but James Lightbody phoned just after six and changed it to ten. They arrived at seven-thirty. I didn't notice the time when they left. It was a busy night. We always give them that table,' she pointed to the table at the very back of the restaurant, where conversation would not be overheard.

'Did they arrive together?'

Julie screwed up her face. 'No, no. They didn't. Georgia arrived first with Joss – the Montpelliers. Joss was in good form, actually. Then ...'

'Why do you say that Joss was in good form? Wasn't he usually?'

Julie brushed her hair back again. Choosing her words carefully she said, 'You'll find out eventually I suppose. He has dementia. Most of the time he and Georgia cover it up very well, but I've known him ask where the toilets are, though he's been here often. A couple of months ago, when there was just the four men, he forgot he'd just eaten his starter and insisted we were trying to swindle him when the waiter arrived with the main course. At other times he seems quite normal. I've heard he still plays a good hand of bridge. It's very odd. Terrible for Georgia. The others are very loyal to them, very supportive.'

'When did Mr Cox, the man I spoke to you about on the phone, arrive and with whom?'

'He and a lady with long, grey hair were the last to arrive. I don't know her name. He wasn't someone you'd forget, arrogant I'd say. I'm sorry he's dead but…' her voice trailed off.

'Hmm,' Di Falco tried to express understanding without using words. 'And the others at the table were?'

'James and Norma Lightbody, Hugh and Susan Harkins, Kevin and Linda McPhail. No, wait. Susan Harkins didn't come. Hugh was on his own. He said she had a stomach bug, I believe. In the end there were only nine of them.'

'Was there anything unusual that you noticed?'

'Just that there was this extra couple. Amanda!' She called to a tall girl with dark hair cut short and long, shapely legs. While her uniform was conventional it showed off the curves of her figure to perfection. When she approached, Di Falco smiled at her warmly.

Amanda looked apprehensive when Julie told her he was a police officer and asked her to answer his questions as well as she could. 'I'm off now,' she added, turning to Di Falco, 'You'll know where to find me if I can help further.'

'Please sit down,' he said to Amanda, giving her the full Hollywood treatment. 'I'm not going to eat you.' But I wouldn't mind trying, he thought.

Slowly and patiently he put her at her ease. It had been a very busy night, with many summer visitors. She remembered there had been a fuss over the seating. The woman with the long, grey hair had been put between Montpellier and Harkins, but she had said very firmly that she wanted to sit beside her old friend, Mrs Lightbody. Using her finger, Amanda traced an anti-clockwise circle on the table.

'So, in the end, Mr McPhail sat at the top of the table with Mrs Montpellier on his right. Mr Montpellier sat beside his wife, then the younger man, then Mr Harkins at the bottom. Opposite Mr Harkins, yes, it was Mr Lightbody, then Mrs McPhail, then the grey-haired woman, then Mrs Lightbody who was beside Mr McPhail.'

When Di Falco asked what they had been talking about, there seemed little Amanda could offer but snatches of conversations she had overheard while serving came back to her. At the end of the main course, Mr Montpellier had been gesturing strangely, pointing at himself then at McPhail then at himself again, going 'pow, pow, pow' as if shooting. She remembered Mrs Montpellier telling her husband to be quiet. That was a bit later. They'd had quite a lot to drink, eight bottles of wine between nine. She couldn't remember if anyone had markedly more or less than the rest. Wanting to help this fanciable detective, Amanda searched her memory. 'Yes, just after his wife told him to be quiet – I was serving coffee – Mr Montpellier said to Mr McPhail, "We pulled you out of the shit and no one lost in the end." Something like that. Mr McPhail didn't say anything in my hearing but I could see he was, like, really angry.'

'I don't suppose you heard anything about going to play golf?'

Her face lit up. 'Yes, I remember now. I was taking payment off their cards ...'

'They split the bill?'

'Yes. Mr McPhail, Mr Harkins, Mr Lightbody and Mrs Monpellier split it equally.'

'Sorry, I interrupted. About the golf?'

'Mr McPhail said he had his clubs in the car. "The fifteenth then the fourth," he said. Then I think he said "our usual".'

'Do you remember Mr Cox saying anything?'

'He said something about re-living his undergraduate days. Oh yes. He said he was glad he'd had carrots as veg. Why would he say that?'

'My mum says they help you see in the dark. It's an auld wifie's saying. You're sure he said that?'

'Yes. Positive. I thought it was really weird.'

She thought they had left about eleven, but could not be sure. It seemed there was nothing more to be learned from Amanda, apart from the phone numbers of the JB group stored in the restaurant's computer. Di Falco left his card with her, should she think of anything else. From the expression on her face he could see she hoped she did. So did he.

* * *

Flick decided to start with the Lightbodys. They lived in a quietly prosperous street off the Canongate.

The house was a snowcemmed bungalow with an immaculate front garden, unimaginatively laid out, all straight lines, grass and pansies. A spotless, white Golf sat on a monoblock driveway in front of an equally spotless, white fold-down garage door. A woman with a pale, unlined complexion answered the door. Her ash-blonde hair had obvious grey roots. 'What do you want?' she asked, her voice world-weary but assured. Showing no surprise at a visit from the police, she confirmed that she was Mrs Norma Lightbody and showed Flick and Di Falco into a tidy but to Flick's eye tasteless, sitting room. The predominant colour pink, with obviously reproduction furniture, it was cluttered with twee ornaments and framed family photographs. A vase containing plastic flowers sat on a bookcase precisely filled with hardback volumes of literary classics. There was nothing irregular or shabby to suggest that any of them had been read.

'You'll be here about the murder,' Norma Lightbody stated. 'We were appalled. Absolutely appalled. He was a very nice young man. I'll go and find my husband.' Despite her words, she gave no hint of emotional engagement in the tragedy. Leaving the officers on a surprisingly lumpy sofa, Mrs Lightbody sailed serenely out of the room to fetch her husband.

Minutes later a short, thin man with a full head of grey hair and a prominent nose entered. His face was tanned and wrinkled. Everything about him was neat and precise, though there was a nervous energy about his movements. Comparing them, it appeared to Flick that all life's troubles had passed her by only to become etched on her husband's features. She thought of *The Picture of Dorian Gray*. When he spoke, his voice was clipped. 'Sorry to keep you, I've been lagging my pipes. I'm James Lightbody.'

He seemed a most unlikely Jolly Boy. It crossed Flick's mind that the moniker might be sarcastic. He sat down facing the officers, his wife pulling in an upright chair beside him.

'I assume you're here because of the murder?' he asked.

Flick introduced herself and Di Falco. 'We understand that you dined with …'

'Just a minute,' Lightbody interrupted, 'I'd like to see your warrants, please.'

Flick had already flashed hers in front of his wife but they duly produced them. He got up, polished his glasses and examined them closely.

'You can't be too careful,' he said as he sat down.

Flick smiled politely and continued. While she asked the questions, Di Falco took notes. 'We understand that you dined at The Adamson last night and that Eric Cox was at your table.'

Lightbody nodded. 'Indeed, Inspector.'

'Could you explain how that came about and what happened after you left the restaurant?'

'Well there's a group of us who meet up regularly. We've been friends for years, since university in most cases. More than thirty years ago there was a tragedy. One of our number, Peter Waldron, murdered Tony

Spencer. My wife has kept in close touch with Mary Spencer, Tony's widow. She moved away but Norma has given her wonderful support for years.' He patted his wife's hand. 'Mary phoned on Wednesday to say she was coming to St Andrews to demonstrate against Waldron's release from prison. Apparently he has terminal cancer ...'

'At least that's the story,' his wife cut in.

'Anyway we, we call ourselves the JBs, were due to dine together last night. Norma asked Mary if she wanted to join us. She said yes but wanted to bring along Eric Cox. He was helping her to publicise her protest. He managed to book into the same B and B in North Castle Street that she is staying in. They were planning another protest today. So they both came and we had a very pleasant evening with no indication that something terrible would happen later.'

'When did you leave the restaurant?'

He furrowed his brow as if thinking deeply. 'Perhaps about eleven.'

'Where did you go then?'

'We finished up at the Harkins' flat on The Scores. They have a lovely ground floor flat with a fine walled garden.'

'We all went there,' his wife emphasised.

'I had a bit of a sore head this morning,' he said, rubbing his forehead for effect. 'Hugh and Susan have always been generous hosts.'

'I believe Mrs Harkins wasn't at the restaurant?'

'Correct,' he said. 'A tummy upset, I believe.'

'But she was feeling better by the time we got back,' she added.

'And when did you leave the flat?'

'Is that relevant? I understand you have a man in custody already.'

'That's as may be, sir. We need to know as much as possible. Would you be good enough to answer the question?'

'I don't remember exactly. It would have been well after midnight.' His wife nodded agreement.

'And how did you get home?'

'We walked. It was a fine night and the fresh air did us good.'

'Particularly you,' his wife added.

'What about the rest of them?'

'We all left about the same time, apart from Mary Spencer. I can't remember exactly.'

'The McPhails definitely left with us,' his wife said. 'Linda and I were arranging to meet for coffee next week. We are going to go to Cupar to get away from the Lammas Fair.'

'Of course, that starts on Monday,' Flick said. The Lammas Fair was heartily disliked by many St Andreans, particularly those of a staid disposition. Centuries-old, it occupied the main streets of the town, giving pleasure to many but causing disturbance and inconvenience to local residents. A market with a variety of stalls that had started the previous day in Market Street was augmented on the Monday and

Tuesday of the next week by fairground attractions, hoop-la, thrill rides and the like, in South Street.

'What about Mary Spencer?' Flick asked.

'She left much earlier,' Norma Lightbody said quickly.

'Did you say she was staying in a B and B in North Castle Street?'

'Yes. She left well before midnight. She insisted on walking back there.' Norma Lightbody leaned forward earnestly.

'On her own?'

'Oh yes.' She shrugged, looking doubtful.

'Did no one offer to escort her?' Flick turned to her husband. 'With the market in town, there are people about we don't usually see in St Andrews.'

He looked indignant. 'I offered of course, but she was adamant. It was just up the road, not a long way.'

'Do you know if she's still in town?'

Norma Lightbody spoke. 'Yes. We've been in touch by mobile phone. She's devastated by Eric's death, utterly devastated. I've invited her here for supper. I was just about to make a lasagne when you called,' she added pointedly.

'Please give us her number before we go. How did the McPhails get home? I believe they live out the High Strathkinness Road.'

'They were going to call a taxi,' James Lightbody said quickly.

'Can you remember if Eric Cox left before or after you?'

The Lightbodys exchanged puzzled looks that would have disgraced most amateur dramatic societies. 'After us, I think,' he said. She nodded vigorously.

'The Montpelliers?'

Puzzled looks were accompanied by head-scratching. 'Before us,' they said in unison. 'Joss was tired,' she added.

'How were they going to get home?'

'Georgia had the car. She had only one glass of wine,' she emphasised.

Flick asked, 'Why do you think Mrs Harkins wasn't at the restaurant? Was her tummy upset genuine?'

The Lightbodys exchanged looks. 'I wondered if it was just an excuse,' she said. 'She might not have wanted to see Mary Spencer.'

'So you think the excuse wasn't genuine?' Flick asked.

'Some people say that she caused all the trouble years ago, but I don't suppose you need to know that.'

Flick noted how she distanced herself from the gossip she longed to impart. 'It would be helpful to know as much as possible. We'll use the information with discretion.'

'Well Susan Harkins has always been, well, wayward.' She used the word as if it had only just occurred to her. 'She was married to Peter Waldron but had an affair with Tony Spencer. It got quite serious. Waldron killed Tony out of jealousy. She divorced him and then she married Hugh, who had been Waldron's partner, and there have been more rumours ...' She shook her head disapprovingly. 'And her daughter, bad blood some people say, but I think, being charitable, it must have been very difficult for her. She looked like Peter Waldron, so there was no doubt there. But she was wayward, like her mother, and insisted on marrying, well, a plumber. And if what we've heard is true, she's married a murderer, just like her mother. Do you have a strong case against him?'

'We can't divulge that, Mrs Lightbody,' Flick said. 'But why did you go back to the Harkins' flat when Mrs Harkins claimed to be unwell?'

'Hugh said he wanted to check on her.'

'And it was convenient for the restaurant,' Lightbody added.

'Was there anything unusual said or done before you split up?'

'Not at all,' she said.

'What were you talking about?'

'We, the ladies, were complaining about the Lammas Fair, I remember. And just general chat. The men were talking, about golf I think.' She looked towards her husband.

'Yes, golf,' he said. 'The Open,' he added.

'Now, if we might have Mary Spencer's mobile number?'

'Of course.' From her tone she might have been allowing a child to have a sweetie. Unhurried, she left the room then came back with a Filofax. Looking at

Di Falco, she dictated the number slowly and with accentuated clarity, as if he had writing difficulties.

Flick smiled at them. 'Thank you very much. Now we should go. Is there anything else?' she asked, turning to Di Falco.

That was his cue. 'What about the golf?' he asked Lightbody.

'The men were discussing the Open, specifically how well Jordan Spieth has done this year.'

'Not that golf. The golf that Mr Cox played with you shortly before he was murdered.'

Lightbody's mouth opened but no sound came out. His wife raised her eyebrows.

'Sir?' Di Falco stared at him.

'Who told you about that?'

'That's not your concern. So there was something to tell about?'

Lightbody shifted in his chair and looked round the room, anywhere but at the officers.

Flick said, 'You are a solicitor, I believe, Mr Lightbody. You know you have a duty to assist the police with our inquiries.'

Taking a deep breath, Lightbody spoke quietly. 'We shouldn't have done it. It'll probably be against some by-law. But we'd all had a bit to drink, and when we get together, we forget our age. We used to get up to some high jinks when we were young. Egged each other on, you know. For some years, after our summer dinner, we have sneaked onto the Old Course and played a couple of holes. Usually this is done in June.

It's amazing how your eyes become accustomed to the dark, and if there's a moon, you can see a surprising amount. Anyway, this June the course was being carefully guarded before the Open so we didn't try. But last night, Kevin McPhail had brought clubs and balls daubed with luminous paint. And we went out and played two holes. Eric Cox came with us.'

'What holes did you play?'

'The fifteenth then the fourth of the Old.'

'How did you get out there? We're not interested in road traffic matters. This is a murder inquiry.'

Lightbody wrung his hands and screwed up his face, the deep wrinkles reminding Di Falco of some exotic, over-bred dog at Crufts. He said quietly, 'Kevin McPhail drove us in his Merc.'

'Who is us?'

'The men: me, Kevin, Joss Montpellier, Hugh Harkins and Eric Cox.'

'When did you do this?'

'We went straight from the restaurant and parked in the Eden car park. The whole thing must have taken about an hour and a half. Even with torches it wasn't easy. But it was fun. Then we joined the ladies at the Harkins' flat.'

'And had Mary Spencer left by the time you got there?'

He nodded.

Flick turned to his wife. 'Why did you go back to the Harkins' flat when you knew Mrs Harkins wasn't keen on meeting Mrs Spencer?'

Lightbody replied quickly. 'We didn't know then that she had made up an excuse not to go to the restaurant. We really thought that with the passage of time they'd at least be able to be polite to one another. Mary Spencer had thought Susan would be at the restaurant, yet she'd come. Linda suggested someone should check on Susan and the flat was convenient for the restaurant and the golf. Hugh gave Linda his key.' He turned to his wife. 'You said when you went in you found Susan in front of the TV with a glass of wine. Mary Spencer saw there had been nothing wrong with her and left almost immediately.'

She nodded. 'It was clear that she'd made up an excuse not to go to the restaurant. Mary saw that she hadn't been prepared to try to be polite. I could see she was furious.'

Flick stared into Lightbody's eyes. 'So you lied to us earlier when you said you had offered to walk her back to where she was staying?'

Looking miserable, he nodded again. His wife's cheeks reddened.

'Why?' Flick asked.

He shrugged. 'I don't know.'

Flick leaned forward. 'I think you do. And unless we get your full cooperation this discussion will continue at Cupar Police Office. Now, the truth please if you want to avoid being charged with an attempt to pervert the course of justice.'

'That's preposterous.'

Flick looked at him steadily then turned to Di Falco. 'Ring for a marked car to transport two persons to Cupar. Tell them to sound their siren.'

'Blues and twos. Right, ma'am.' Di Falco produced his mobile.

'James!' Norma Lightbody reacted as Flick knew she would.

'All right,' her husband said. 'It's just that this golf business is a bit embarrassing. We occupy a certain position, you know …'

'Right,' Flick said. 'Now, the order in which people left the flat?'

Sullenly, Lightbody said, 'Well Mary Spencer was first, as I said. When we got back from the golf, Cox came in with us and joined us in a dram. We all left about the same time.'

Di Falco leaned forward. 'That's not what you said earlier. You said he'd left after you.'

Lightbody shrugged. 'I'm sorry. I'm a bit confused. He got up to go when we did. And the McPhails did leave with us, and yes, Kevin was going to drive. He can take his drink, you know. He wouldn't have been a real danger. Georgia Montpellier took Joss home shortly before Cox left. I genuinely don't know what the time was.'

'It was ten past two when we got home. I remember looking at the clock,' his wife said. He frowned.

Flick asked, 'Did Mr Cox have any disagreement with anyone last night?'

They looked at each other then said 'No' in unison.

'Very well. Now, please tell us what was said at the Adamson that annoyed Mr McPhail.'

'I don't know about that,' Lightbody said quickly.

'I understand you were sitting next to Mr McPhail,' Di Falco said to his wife, 'so please tell us.' He had not put his phone away and held it as if he was about to punch in a number.

Her eyes opened wide and strayed round the room. 'Joss, Mr Montpellier, was being silly. Something about Czechoslovakia, I think …' she paused, seeking inspiration.

Her husband cut in. 'We hadn't wanted to bring this up, Inspector, but Joss Montpellier has dementia. It's not too bad, as yet. Some days he can be his old self, at other times very silly and forgetful. It's terribly sad. Georgia, his wife, has a difficult time of it and we try to support her in any way we can. Kevin McPhail isn't always as patient as he might be.'

'And did Mr Montpellier say something about getting Mr McPhail out of the shit?' Di Falco looked directly at Norma Lightbody.

Her blush intensified and she glanced at her husband. Taking her cue from his grim expression, she shook her head. 'I don't remember that.'

'Really?' Di Falco did not hide his scepticism.

'Absolutely.'

Flick exchanged looks with Di Falco then said, 'We have caught you out lying to us. Repeatedly. That is a serious matter. Now I want you to concentrate very hard and tell me if anything unusual was said or done last night apart from what you have told us. Or anything that might cast a light on Mr Cox's murder. If you don't tell us now and we subsequently find out you've concealed something material, you will be charged with an attempt to pervert the course of justice. I don't need to spell out how serious that would be for you. Sir.' The pause before she said 'sir' made it almost insulting.

Neither said anything. After waiting a full minute, Flick said, 'We'll see ourselves out.'

In the car, Flick asked, 'Was that just embarrassment over the illegal golf and Montpellier's dementia, or is there more under the surface?'

'It could be embarrassment, ma'am. Appearances are very important to them. But for my money, something odd's been going on.'

She said, 'And if it has, does it have anything to do with the murder? It's been a long day, but I think we should see Mary Spencer before she gets weighed down by the Lightbody's lasagne and whatever's said while she eats it. Phone her mobile.'

* * *

Mary Spencer was at her B and B when Di Falco phoned. They went straight over to see her. The landlady's brusque manner showed her disapproval of guests who got themselves murdered, perhaps without paying their bill, Flick thought, and during the busiest time of year too.

'So can I clean his room and let it out tomorrow?' she asked. 'A policeman took away all Mr Cox's stuff this afternoon but said I had to get your permission to do anything to the room.'

Flick promised to let her know the following day and they were shown up to Mary Spencer's room. As they stood outside the door they heard a woman's voice. '… right, well … okay. I'll see you later.' Flick rapped the door and entered as soon as the voice said 'Hello?'

The grey-haired lady she had seen with the placard the previous day was sitting on the bed, her mobile phone beside her. She looked guilty, as if she had been caught doing something wrong. A shapeless sweater covered large, sagging breasts. Her trousers were stained and robust shoes needed a clean. As she reached to put her phone into a capacious and battered handbag, Flick observed rough, strong hands engrained with dirt and nails bitten to the quick.

Sensing someone easily spooked into nervous antagonism, Flick sat on a chair, smiled and made introductions. Trying to be non-threatening, Di Falco stood by the bay window which gave spectacular views of the sea, the ruined castle and some way down The Scores. At first, Mary Spencer gave brief, direct answers to Flick's questions. After Tony's murder she had gone to live north of Inverness at Culbokie; she had been brought up on the Black (pronounced Blaack) Isle. She lived alone in a 'wee croft with some sheep and hens'. She had contacted Eric Cox to support his campaign to keep murderers in prison for life and he had been keen to help her protest about Waldron's early release. She found him to be a 'queer laddie' but 'his heart was in the right place'. Her distress over his death was obviously genuine.

'He understood what I suffered,' she said with feeling. 'Every night I go to bed alone and every morning I wake up, hoping to see Tony's face on the pillow, but he's not there and never will be. It's a life sentence for me, but not for Waldron. And he killed someone else in jail.' Looking at the lined, weatherbeaten face, dark eyes burning with resentment, Flick could see that long ago she might have been pretty. 'Mind you,' Mary continued, 'I blame that wife of his, Susan. She threw herself at Tony. There was nothing between them, not really. Not on his side of it anyway. He told me he loved her but he was just being stupid. And as soon as he'd gone she threw herself at Hugh Harkins. And Norma tells me he's not been the last. It's her, not Tony, Waldron should have killed.' The clear, attractive northern lilt seemed at odds with the visceral hatred of her words.

She confirmed that she had demonstrated outside the Smiths' house the previous day, and that she had been moved across the street. 'It was good to see Constable McKellar again. He was really nice and apologetic about getting me away from the door Waldron was behind. I remember him at the trial. The defence QC gave him a hard time but he stuck to his guns.'

She said Norma Lightbody ('she's been a really

good friend') had invited her to join the old group for dinner and had been happy for Eric to come along as well. She confirmed that she had been persuaded to go back to the Harkins' flat, just up The Scores from the R and A, where they would wait for the men, including Eric, to return from their night-time golf. ('Daft, but these boys were always up to capers in the old days.')

She had not stayed long. 'That woman Harkins made me mad. I'd been ready to see her in company, but she'd made up an excuse not to come. I went back to her flat with the others out of interest, and I wasn't impressed, the little I saw of it. I thought she'd be in her bed but she was up. Nothing wrong with her. "Oh Mary," she says, "you look so Highland." There were things I could have said to her but I didn't. And I wanted to be fresh for our protest this morning. So I left. Of course the protest was cancelled.'

Flick asked, 'Did one of the Lightbodys speak to you on the phone before we arrived and tell you what to say to us?'

Mary sat up with a jolt. 'What do you mean?'

'What I say, Please tell us.'

'He told me to tell the truth.'

'And had someone earlier told you to say something else?'

She looked away then nodded.

'Who?'

She sat breathing deeply, eyes down. 'Jimmy. He was always Jimmy back then.'

'Jimmy Lightbody?'

'Yes.'

'What did he tell you to say before he told you to tell the truth?'

'Not to mention the golf … I should say we'd all gone back to the Harkins' flat.'

'And anything else?'

'Such as?'

'Perhaps not to mention Kevin McPhail getting upset at what Joss Montpellier said in the restaurant?'

Clearly confused, Mary stammered. 'Well yes, but I … I don't remember that bit, that's the thing, I really don't. I do remember Joss pretending to shoot at Kevin. I put it down to Joss not being himself, you know?'

'We know he has dementia.'

'Yes, it's awfully sad. But I really don't know what it was all about.'

'But Mr Lightbody didn't want you to talk about it anyway?'

'No. It's kind of embarrassing when he's bad, apparently.'

Flick stared at her in silence. She looked back defiantly. Quietly Flick said, 'Are you not curious why we're asking all these questions?'

Mary gulped. 'I suppose it's a murder …'

'And Mr Lightbody told you we'd have a lot of questions?'

'Well, yes. He said you might.'

'Did he tell you he'd been talking earlier today to the others who'd been at the restaurant?'

'I can't remember. Possibly.'

'Possibly or definitely?'

She seemed to think. 'Well yes. He did say they'd been speaking. I don't know what they said to each other, apart from breaking the bad news,' she added.

'And agreeing a story?'

'Well, yes.'

'But anyway Mr Lightbody phoned you just before we arrived and advised you to tell the truth?'

'Yes.' She looked miserable.

'Mrs Spencer, this is a murder inquiry and it is important that we know as much as possible about what happened last night. Is there anything you haven't told us?'

'No.' She opened her eyes wide, a picture of innocence.

Di Falco turned from the window. 'Did you hear or see anything during the night? An argument, for example?'

'No. It must have happened right in front of my window, but I take sleeping pills and the first I was aware something was wrong was an awful shindy and blue flashing lights when you arrived. I got up and looked out but I had no idea it was Eric …' Her voice caught.

'When do you plan to return home?' Flick asked.

'I'm booked in here till Monday morning. Then I'll take the train north.'

'Fine, but we'll need your address and it's just possible that we'll need you to come back. I hope not,' she added.

The officers left Mary Spencer sitting on the bed, alone, unhappy, resentful and confused.

Flick was exhausted and longed to see Verity. 'Tomorrow,' she said to Di Falco. 'Early.'

8

It had not taken Osborne long to unpack. He looked round the cramped room on the third floor of his B and B. This was not what he had in mind. The polythene bags full of papers lay accusingly on the bed. He would have to do something about them if he was to get paid. He looked at the list of names and contact details Mrs Smith had given him, the so-called Jolly Boys probably. He wanted a heads-up on the business and the old sergeant whom Waldron blamed for verballing him would be the best starting-point. He rummaged among the papers, found a copy of Waldron's indictment and saw from the list of Crown witnesses that the person in question was Detective Sergeant Francis Thomson of Fife Constabulary. Was he still alive and if so, where did he live?

The youth answering the Cupar Police Office telephone was cagey at first. Osborne had to invent a friendship with 'old Tommo' struck up years ago at a conference on inter-jurisdiction cooperation at Milton Keynes and a standing invitation to meet up if ever Osborne came to Fife. In fact Osborne had avoided conferences like the plague, regarding them as jamborees of political correctness, only as good as the hospitality budget. The ruse worked and the youth gave Osborne the address of a flat in a sheltered housing development on the east side of Cupar. 'I heard Mr Thomson's wife died about six months ago,' he added.

A taxi dropped Osborne at the flats. There was an entry phone with the names of the different occupants on a plate. Beside 'Thomson' a bit of paper had been roughly sellotaped. 'Ryder' was written on it. Osborne pushed the button and hoped that his taxi fare would not prove to have been wasted.

A woman's voice answered. Osborne stuck to his 'old friend from the police' line and he was buzzed up. The flat was on the second floor of a spruce modern development, clean and well-kept with a potted Aspidistra on the landing beside the door. A woman in her forties showed Osborne in. Her blouse was sufficiently unbuttoned to reveal generous breasts and when he followed her into the sitting room Osborne's eye was drawn to the blue skirt stretched over an ample bottom.

Thomson himself was sitting watching television. The winner of a golf tournament was receiving his prize. Osborne could see that this octogenarian was good for his age. His figure was still trim. Thin on top, his white hair was quite long at the back and sides. Luxuriant mutton-chop sideburns framed rosy cheeks. His features were sharp and shrewd eyes sized up Osborne who, without being asked, took a seat opposite.

'Do I know you?' Thomson asked, his voice clear with a strong Fife accent.

'My name's Noel Osborne. I used to be a detective inspector in the Met, but I've retired and I've gone freelance. I need to talk to you about the Peter Waldron case,' Osborne said, dropping the 'old friends' line.

'Oh that.' Thomson put his arm behind the woman, who was standing beside his chair. From the look that came over her face Osborne guessed he had just nipped her bottom. 'Would you go and see to the supper, Pet. Mr Osborne and I won't be long. Well?' he said aggressively when she had gone.

'I hear your wife died recently, but ...' Osborne said, trying to put the older man at a disadvantage.

'What the hell am I doing with her?' He glanced at the door through which the woman had left. 'Well it's none of your business but I'll tell you anyway. I nursed my wife, whom I loved very much, for several months before she died. Lena, who showed you in, helped with the nursing. You only live once, as they say, and we fancied each other. We only did something about that after Bea died. Lena has got me taking Viagra and I bet I've had more sex in the last month than you've had in the last year. I'm a new man. The only trouble is that I have to pay for the bloody Viagra. I should get it on the NHS but my GP won't prescribe it. If you're a depressive you get free pills to make you undepressed. If you're normal, why shouldn't you get free pills to make you feel good? Don't you agree? I've nothing to hide, nothing to be ashamed of. Actually

I'm proud of myself; I had her last night when we went to bed and again this morning when we woke up. What about you? When did you last have sex?'

Whatever Osborne had expected it was not this. 'Oh I have a girl in Spain, where I live. We had sex before I left this morning.' This was a lie; Maria had left him a month earlier and was now bestowing her favours on a churro-maker from Fuengirola.

'Yea. Right.' Thomson smiled pityingly at him. 'So has Waldron hired you?'

'Yes. Look, I'm old-school. When I was in the Met I cleaned up the East End. And I didn't do it by acting the bloody choirboy. I knew who the villains were and I went after them. We were allowed to do our fucking jobs then, know what I mean?'

'Are you wired?'

'No. Want to see?'

'Not necessary. Do you have one of these modern mobile phones?'

'Yes.'

'Well go to the kitchen and give it to Lena. I don't understand them but I see on the telly that they do everything but fart and shag. I don't want to be recorded or photographed.'

Osborne got up and found Lena holding a glass of white wine in the well-appointed kitchen. Thomson called from the sitting room, 'Look after his phone, will you, Pet?' 'I'll be back for this,' Osborne said, placing his phone on the table beside her.

'It was a clever verbal,' he said on re-entering the

sitting room. 'A smart guy like Waldron would never have admitted it to you, but this showed his motive and he was slagging off the dead. The jury wouldn't have liked that.'

Thomson smiled, as if Osborne had cracked an unfunny joke. 'He said what I said he said.'

'Even if he did say it, it didn't mean he was the killer.'

'Your point being?'

'They don't need to disprove the verbal to show the conviction was wrong.'

'Of course the conviction was right. No one else had a motive as far as we could see, he kept these poisonous frogs and knew how to deal with them, and he had the murder weapon in his pocket.'

'Would a man like Waldron, not stupid, forget about the murder weapon and leave it in his pocket?'

'Well I didn't plant it.'

'Someone else might have.'

'Like?'

'The real killer. Or one of your squad.'

'Fuck's sake, man. Waldron's a killer. He murdered another prisoner. Had you forgotten that? If there's one thing that makes me sick it's people who did the job as it has to be done then turn into hypocritical wankers. You should draw your pension, buy some Viagra and get a life.' He turned up the volume on the television.

The interview was over. Osborne stood up. Unable to think of an effective response, he stalked out of the room. In the kitchen, he eyed up Lena as she handed back his mobile. She gave him a don't-you-dare look.

Outside the flats, Osborne needed a drink. He walked into the centre of Cupar and found a down-market pub, surprisingly crowded given the good weather. Over a couple of large whiskies, in a corner on his own, he mulled over the day's events. Strange thoughts swirled round his head. His glass was empty. Would he have another scotch? He remembered the saying 'a drink's nice, two's enough and three's not nearly enough' and decided that would be a bad idea. Besides he felt hungry. He pushed his way out of the pub. On the street, his nose twitched at the smell of frying. Across the road was a fish and chip shop where he bought a black pudding supper. Sitting on a car bonnet and enjoying the evening sun, he munched away. The food hit the spot and he went back for an extra poke of chips. Then he took a bus back to St Andrews.

The journey took a quarter of an hour. As he passed fertile grain fields almost ready for harvest, he reached a decision: he would become a crusader for justice. There was money to be made out of it. He'd lost count of the sob stories about innocent people being banged up for years. There were newspaper articles, books, TV programmes and even films about them. Those who helped them were bound to get their cut of the proceeds. And his gut told him that Waldron had not killed Spencer. Out of jail and soon to die, why make such a fuss? He was sure Thomson had verballed him. The killing must have been premeditated and a bright man like Waldron would not have left the murder weapon in one of his pockets. Had Thomson been under pressure to get a result – any result? Or had he genuinely believed Waldron was guilty? Whatever, he had framed an innocent man but he would never admit it. When Osborne had cleaned up the East End he'd only fitted up those he knew were villains. An unfamiliar feeling of moral superiority swept over him and he rather liked it. As for the murder Waldron had committed, kicking to death a paedophile in jail deserved time off for good behaviour in his book.

When he got out at the bus station he fumbled in his pockets and found the list of names Mrs Smith had given him. He was supposed to give daily updates and had nothing to show for his trip to Cupar. And he wanted to get paid. He studied the list, comparing the names with the notes he had scribbled on the back of his air ticket. At the top were Joss and Georgia Montpellier. They lived in a house called Melville in Hepburn Gardens. The friendly woman in the ticket office gave him directions and pointed out a bus soon to go in that direction.

The driver helpfully showed him where to get off and the street, Lawhead Road East, he should walk down to reach Hepburn Gardens, where he should turn left. Five minutes later he was staring at the house named Melville. A six-foot wooden fence backed by densely-planted conifers shielded it from the road. He opened the heavy wooden gate and walked down the thinly-gravelled driveway which twisted left then right, revealing a large, stone house, spookily shaded by more conifers. There were lawns on both sides of the driveway before it widened into a space for cars to turn.

He felt a blow to the side of his head. Momentarily stunned, he turned to fight back but there was no one near.

'Sorry, old chap. Didn't see you or I'd have shouted fore.' The patrician voice came from a shadowed area on the far side of the lawn to his left. The speaker was a tall, thin man with a good head of black hair. His navy blue sweater looked as if it had been made for someone bulkier. As he walked jerkily towards him, Osborne could see that his clothes were scruffy. He carried an iron golf club in one hand but there was nothing menacing in his demeanour. 'Do I know you?' the man asked.

'I'm Noel Osborne,' he replied, rubbing his head. He saw the golf ball that had hit him lying on the gravel beside him. 'That hurt.'

'I said I'm sorry. I was practising my pitching. What are you doing here anyway?'

'Are you Joss Montpellier?'

'Of course I am.'

'I'm here to ask you some questions about Peter Waldron.'

Montpellier bent to pick up his ball. He stared at Osborne, a puzzled look on his face. 'Peter Waldron? He's in jail.'

'He's out.'

'Out? He must have escaped. Good Lord.' He paused, looked round. 'I don't think he's here.'

It had been a long day and Osborne was in no mood for a smart-arse. 'Don't take the piss. I'm serious.'

Montpellier scratched his head, tousling his hair. He stared at Osborne, who sensed incomprehension, panic and aggression. 'I don't know what you mean.'

He's lost his marbles, Osborne thought; gently does it, I might still get something out of him. He smiled, he hoped reassuringly, and said, 'Do you remember he was convicted of murder?'

'Yes.' Montpellier sounded indignant.

'Do you think he did it?'

A silly smile spread across the tall man's sunburned face. He shook his head but said nothing.

'Did you like him?'

Montpellier frowned. 'Good company, but too clever for his own good.' He thought for a moment then added in a confidential whisper, 'I didn't like that fellow Spencer, the one he was supposed to have killed. Slippery as an eel, I always thought. And he drank too much. Very indiscreet.'

'Who else had a motive to kill Spencer?'

'Search me. Any number of chaps he'd cuckolded, maybe.'

'What about the rest of your group, the Jolly Boys?'

'We all stuck together. Helped each other out, know what I mean? What friends are for.'

'How did you help each other?'

'The kid could never have afforded to ditch Kidwife One if it hadn't been for us.'

This was getting interesting. Waldron had mentioned someone called the kid. 'What did you do to help him?'

The silly smile came back but was wiped off his face by a shout of 'Joss!' A tall woman with a regal bearing came from the house. As she approached, Osborne could see sharp features under heavy make-up and bottle-blackened hair, lacquered to withstand the strongest gale the North Sea might throw at her. She was immaculately dressed in tailored red trousers and a blue linen shirt. She had retained a good figure and had a haughtiness that commanded attention. 'Who are you?' she asked coldly.

'Noel Osborne. I ...'

Montpellier interrupted excitedly. 'Peter Waldron's escaped from jail. He's been asking about him.'

The woman closed her eyes and took a deep breath. 'Are you a journalist?' she demanded, curling her lip.

Osborne drew himself up to his full height. 'Yes, I'm doing a feature on Peter Waldron and I would very much like to hear your side of the story.' He had worked out that the Jolly Boys would be unlikely to want to speak to a detective hired by Waldron.

The woman frowned. Her eyebrows were painted on with no hair underneath and this diminished what would have been a killer glare. 'Well I have no intention of telling you anything. Kindly clear off from here. And please don't trouble me or my husband again. I don't know what he's been telling you, but I'm sure you can see he's not himself. You'd be most unwise to rely on anything he's said.'

Montpellier hung his head, chastened. Osborne saw he was going to gain nothing by extending his visit. 'Well tell him to stop firing golf balls at visitors,' he snapped then turned on his heel.

'It's dinner time, Joss,' the woman said, more gently.

'I thought we'd had it,' came the reply.

Osborne didn't look back. For the first time he sensed that he might be getting somewhere. If only that woman had not interrupted. He checked his notes and the list of addresses. Kevin McPhail was the kid. According to Waldron, his wife (Kidwife One?) was called Hannah. On Amy Smith's list, his wife's name was Linda and he lived in a house called Viewmount on the High Strathkinness Road. He found the taxi company's card and called them.

Quarter of an hour later he was dropped off on high ground to the west of the town outside one of a row of 1930s-style white houses with flat roofs. In the driveway, a large Mercedes sat. Highly-polished and bearing the number plate KMP 504, it was a clear statement of wealth. Osborne wondered how old the car actually was and why, if McPhail was really wealthy, he did not have a grander house. Parked almost apologetically, in a corner of the driveway close to a rhododendron and just failing to block access to the garage, was a small Fiat. It was mud-spattered, with an obvious scratch above the rear wheel but had an up-to-date registration number. The house's main door was shut and there was no sign of life at the front. Osborne's finger hovered over the bell then he decided to snoop round the back.

Creeping along a narrow grass path, he heard voices. Stealthily, he peered round a corner through untrimmed Jasmine. On a patio to the rear of the house two men and two women sat in a semi-circle, drinking and enjoying the balmy evening. From their position they could gaze over sand-coloured grain fields towards the sea. The scent of flowers from the garden mingled with cigarette smoke. One of the men was talking: 'He's a liability. It's funny in a pathetic way, but you never know what he's going to come out with.'

'It's a shame. He was damn clever in his day,' the second man, the smoker, said. 'And jolly discreet,' he added.

'It drives Georgia up the wall,' the elder of the women said in a languid voice. Osborne could see she had grey hair cut short. Her face was round and she wore rimless glasses. She too was smoking.

'I saw he and Cox were talking a lot last night, at dinner and during the golf.' The second man had his back to Osborne. He was bald and had a habit of shrugging his left shoulder as he spoke, as if to emphasise what he was saying.

'He was talking a load of crap,' the first man said firmly, brushing a lock of straw-coloured hair out of his eyes so that it lay across the top of his scalp.

'Don't you ever get like that, Kev,' the other woman said, rising to offer crisps. Osborne guessed she was about forty, perhaps twenty years younger than the others. She wore a blue and white striped top and white jeans which showed off her good figure. She had shoulder-length dark hair and a long face with a small mouth. Her upper teeth showed when she talked. Her accent was distinctively Scottish.

'If I do, please give me a pill,' the first man said. 'Now, who's for a re-fill?' He got up and carried two glasses into the house. Paunchy, with a brick-coloured face, the open neck of his Hawaiian-style shirt revealed a gold chain and grey chest hair.

As he returned with the re-fills, Osborne sneezed. The sneeze, brought on by the pollen in the air, had taken him by surprise and he had been unable to stifle it. The man dropped one of the glasses which shattered, sending fragments of glass and ice skidding across the patio.

All four turned towards him. Osborne knew he must appear confident. 'I hope I'm not interrupting anything,' he said breezily as he walked forward and stood in front of the semi-circle.

The first man, who had to be McPhail, set down the unspilled drink and stood facing him, hands on hips. 'Just what the hell do you think you're doing?'

'I'm a journalist, an investigative journalist, and

I'm doing a piece on Peter Waldron. I need your side of the story.'

'Well you're not getting it.'

'That would be a shame. "A conspiracy of silence" always seems so suspicious. Waldron still says he was framed, probably by a so-called friend. It'll make a good feature: "My thirty-one years of hell", I think I'll call it. If you don't talk to me it'll be very one-sided. Totally one-sided, actually.' He paused and looked from one to another. 'I believe both you gentlemen are Jolly Boys?' There was no response. 'Mr McPhail, obviously, and Mr Lightbody or Mr Harkins?'

'Harkins.' The bald man shrugged his shoulder as he spoke.

Osborne turned to the grey-haired woman. 'So Mrs Susan Harkins, formerly Mrs Waldron? Do you believe your first husband murdered Anthony Spencer?'

She squirmed in her chair. A blush showed under her make-up. 'I said all I have to say years ago.' She had an unlined face, prominent lips and long eyelashes. Her pink, calf-length trousers and top were well-coordinated without perhaps being expensive. Rings glittered on her small fingers. Osborne thought she looked like a middle-class tart.

'You were having an affair with Spencer, weren't you? Did you want rid of him permanently? And your husband as well? You could have laid your hands on the poisonous frog any time and put the golf tee into your husband's pocket.'

Harkins jumped up, fists clenched. 'How dare you? That's my wife you're accusing.' Osborne stood his ground. He had been confronted by angry men before and could tell from the flickering eyes and the stiff, straight arms that this man probably hadn't been in a fight since school days. If then.

His wife said sharply, 'Hugh don't. You'll make matters worse.' He took a step back and unclenched his fists. A look of relief flashed across his face.

Osborne said, 'I'm not accusing her, just pointing out. Waldron going down didn't do you any harm, did it? You finished up with his wife.'

'Neither of us had anything to do with Spencer's death.'

'So you say. But what were Cox and Montpellier talking about last night? Might Montpellier have spilled the beans about what really happened to Spencer? Pity we can't ask Cox because he's been murdered.'

McPhail cut in. 'I've had enough of this. If you don't leave now, I'll call the police. And if you print anything defamatory, by God I'll make you pay for it.'

Adrenaline was flowing through Osborne; he was enjoying himself. In no mood to stop rattling cages, he turned to McPhail. 'They called you the kid, didn't they? I bet you got pissed off with that. What was it that the other Jolly Boys did for you so you could afford her?' He nodded towards the younger woman. 'I assume you're Kidwife Two? Linda?'

When Osborne had rattled cages as a cop, there

had usually been a burly constable present to protect him. On this St Andrews patio he was alone and outnumbered. Enraged, McPhail punched him hard on the jaw. Osborne's instincts kicked in. Viciously, he kneed McPhail in the balls and as he doubled up caught his nose with an uppercut, cracking a cartilage. As McPhail tried to staunch the blood and Harkins stood by indecisively, Osborne decided to leave. 'I'll want answers. I'll be back,' he shouted over his shoulder.

Away from the house and seeing no one in pursuit, he phoned for a taxi and waited. At the same time as the taxi, a marked police car arrived. It was the police car that took Osborne away.

9

'I took a gigot chop out of the freezer for you, Bagawath,' Cynthia Arbuthnot said, a smile on her lips but not in her eyes.

Baggo Chandavarkar had been wondering why there were only three mouth-watering sirloin steaks marinading in a dish while the coals of the barbeque began to turn grey. 'Thank you, but I do eat beef. I'm what you might call a slightly lapsed Hindu.' He grinned but her smile remained frozen, revealing a smudge of bright red lipstick on her front teeth. It had been a fine, warm day in Edinburgh and when Baggo and Melanie arrived at her parents' house, a short walk up the hill from her flat, her father, Sheriff Charles Arbuthnot who presided over the court in Airdrie, was on the south-facing patio of their substantial house, all set to display what he considered to be his cooking prowess on the barbeque. A gin and tonic in his hand and a voluminous white apron covering his large stomach, he was in expansive form. Obviously having fun, he poked fussily at the coals to see if they were ready.

'And did you prepare the marinade, Dad?' Melanie asked innocently.

'I left that to the sous-chef,' he replied, a twinkle in his eye.

'And the salad?'

'She did that too,' he admitted.

'As usual,' her mother said, this time her eyes smiling as well as her lips. 'And I put the chocolate in the bananas and wrapped them in tin-foil.'

'Your garden is looking beautiful,' Baggo said, admiring the colourful herbaceous border. 'I hear you do it yourselves. You must have green fingers.'

'Thank you,' Cynthia said. 'Would you like a quick tour while Gordon Ramsay does his stuff?'

Surprised by the invitation, Baggo left Melanie with her father. His industrial-strength gin and tonic topped up, he followed Cynthia up the side of the border, pausing as she pointed out different flowers. She was still a good-looking woman, he thought, though some would say she should lose weight. Might Melanie look like her thirty years down the line? He wouldn't mind if she did.

'I can see you love your garden,' he said.

'I do. I find working with my plants very therapeutic.'

'I understand. When my mother is worried about something she bakes.'

Cynthia nodded. 'I always feel better after an afternoon in the garden, even if I stiffen up later. But look, I can't control everything here. A bird must have dropped a Phlox seed beside that Geum, that one with the orange flower. The Phlox is windolene pink and the two colours clash. I'll have to move one. They're both good, strong plants but they just don't go together.' She turned to him. 'Can you not see that?'

Was the double meaning deliberate or subconscious, Baggo wondered. 'Today some artists would say the contrast works,' he replied.

She sighed. 'A lot of us find it hard to get used to the modern ways. Once ideas become rooted in childhood we find it difficult to uproot them.'

'Gardens change and evolve. An old plant that ceases to be beautiful should be dug out and that can be hard work. It is the same with ideas.'

Taking him by surprise, she put her hand, hot and knarled with arthritis, on his arm. 'I know you're a good man, Bagawath. I know that. My husband and I will try to dig out our old plants, but whatever happens, please never make my daughter unhappy.'

Disinhibited by gin, her voice caught and she looked at him earnestly.

'Mrs Arbuthnot, please believe me, that is the last thing I would wish to do.'

'That is reassuring. Thank you. But I'm still going to move that Phlox. Now, if you prefer, I'll take the lamb gigot and you can have my steak. We'd better get back. The great chef can get quite temperamental if people don't come and eat when he's ready.'

A shout of 'Service!' came from the patio. They exchanged hesitant grins and went to take their seats round the weathered teak garden table.

'So how's your swotting going for your inspector's

exam, Bagawath?' Charles Arbuthnot asked after the ritual expressions of praise for the chef.

'As well as can be expected, thank you sir. But I had a welcome interruption. An old friend from my days in Wimbledon CID dropped in for coffee. She lives in St Andrews and was here to inform the next of kin in a murder, always a horrible job. She came to see me after she had done it. The next of kin lives near here I believe, a Mrs Cox. Perhaps you know her?'

Charles looked puzzled.

'Of course we do,' Cynthia said. 'She lives in Midmar Drive. Good Lord, was it her son who died?'

'Yes. Yesterday he had been demonstrating against the release of a murderer and he was found dead in the early hours this morning.'

Melanie said, 'You didn't tell me. I remember Eric Cox. He was at the bar for a while. He was an oddball. But murdered ...'

'I saw him on the News last night. Was it Peter Waldron he had been demonstrating against?' Charles asked.

'I believe so,' Baggo replied.

'Gracious me. I was his junior counsel at his trial. He'd asked for me specially. He was a solicitor and had instructed me a few times. He was supposed to have poisoned a chap who'd been sleeping with his wife. He was found guilty but I didn't believe he'd done it. You know our system is tilted so it gives the benefit of the doubt to the accused, and a lot of guilty men walk free. You know that better than anyone,' he said to Baggo. 'But when you defend someone who goes down and you think they're innocent it's a terrible feeling. This case was worse as he'd wanted me to represent him. Of course it was my senior who did all the work, and he did it competently, I thought, but I felt terrible for a long time afterwards.'

'They've arrested Waldron's son-in-law. The fiscal insisted on charging him, but my friend, an inspector, is far from being convinced of his guilt.'

Charles said, 'Waldron was verballed, cleverly. It made me very angry. He should not have gone down.' His face clouded, he shot a glance at Baggo then continued, 'He had a daughter. She was very young at the time of the trial. It must be her husband who's accused. Poor girl.'

The silence that followed was awkward.

Swallowing a mouthful of robust Argentinian Malbec, Baggo said, 'In the police, we hate seeing guilty men escape justice, but we have got used to it; I suppose it is the price of a civilised society. Some officers fit up known criminals, regardless of whether they actually committed the crime they are charged with. If they are bad eggs they deserve it, that is the justification. My old boss in Wimbledon, Inspector No we called him, had no scruples about that. "I only pot villains, but by God I pot them, and it doesn't matter what for," he would say.' Melanie scowled, partly at what Baggo had just said, partly at his attempt at a cockney accent. He continued, 'But there is no excuse for inventing evidence against a genuinely innocent man, even if you believe him to be guilty.'

Charles looked steadily at him. 'I hope you really mean that, Bagawath.' Turning towards the garden, he sighed. 'You know, murder trials have always had a special atmosphere, even now that life doesn't mean life. They arouse strong emotions and are particularly difficult for the courts as there is always one important witness missing, the deceased. Not that Spencer probably had much idea who scraped his arm with the poisoned golf tee. But another factor is the tendency to look at the deceased through rose-tinted spectacles. The verbal they gave Waldron had him speaking ill of the dead, and that didn't help with the jury.'

'I can see how that must have been very tough for you, sir,' Baggo said.

'Bananas filled with chocolate,' Cynthia said brightly, changing the subject. As she served the sweet, mushy dessert that had been warming on the barbeque, Charles refilled the wine glasses. Melanie asked about shows they planned to see in the Edinburgh Festival and the mood lightened.

'We'll tidy up and get coffee,' Cynthia said pointedly to Melanie when they had finished eating. The women left the two men together. Charles poured more wine and they sat back, looking out over the garden as the light faded. Baggo wondered what was coming.

Charles broke the silence. 'We're Cynthia and

Charles, Bagawath. Please drop the "sir" and "Mrs Arbuthnot".'

'Thank you, er, Charles. But everyone calls me Baggo.'

'Baggo it is then.' He paused. 'We're terribly proud of Melanie, you know.'

'And so you should be.'

'I read once that when someone says they are proud of their offspring they are often complimenting themselves for bringing them up well. But we are proud of her.'

'She is a remarkable person. I've heard it said that some people look at their children and admire themselves.' As soon as he had said this he regretted it, but Charles laughed.

'I haven't heard that one before. It's good. And apt. I was delighted when Melanie decided to become an advocate. The bar is very different to what it was like in my day. Much more competitive, harder to make a good living. But the glass ceiling has been well and truly shattered so women can and do get to the top. I think Melanie might do so. If she is given the opportunity and not thwarted.' He sniffed nervously, making his face twitch. His concern for his daughter was almost palpable.

'I would never try to thwart her. She is used to the stimulation and challenge of her work and could not now do without it. She is lucky to enjoy what she does,' he added.

'I agree. A lot of people don't enjoy their jobs. But

it's difficult for a woman to pursue a successful career and be a wife and mother. Of course, men are much more hands-on around the house than they used to be. Do you do your bit of the housework?'

Baggo gulped. 'Melanie knows how she likes things, but yes, I do help her, hoovering, making the bed and so on.' The reference to bed-making made Charles wince. Baggo continued lightly, 'She enjoys my curries, when I cook, but is not so fond of my omelettes. They are too leathery, she says.'

Charles didn't smile. He leaned forward with another sniff. 'Do you encounter any difficulty because you are living with a white woman? Excuse me for asking, but I need to know.' The barbeque chef's affable veneer had been stripped away. He was now in sheriff mode.

The directness took Baggo aback. 'No, not really. We get the odd unfriendly look and there's the occasional remark it's best to ignore but our friends think nothing of it. Times have changed, I am glad to say.' He looked defiantly at Charles' impassive face and sensed racism. 'Does it bother you?' he asked coldly.

'It really doesn't. I've asked myself that. The simple fact that you are Indian does not concern me. It's not how I imagined Melanie's life working out, but if you're right for her, fine. What does concern me is the difficulty inherent in a couple having vastly different backgrounds and cultures. And you will encounter racial prejudice, sometimes subtle, sometimes blatant.' Baggo frowned. Charles took a mouthful of wine. 'Let me tell you about a case I had a few years ago. An Asian boy was out with his white girlfriend. Four youths you might call white trash chased him up a close where they kicked him so badly that the witness who found him said there was so much blood that he couldn't tell what colour he was. That blatantly racist assault made my blood boil and when they were convicted I gave them all five years.' He sniffed. 'The Appeal Court reduced it to four years. I do not believe that I am racist. But I want the best for my daughter and with you there will be difficulties ...' His voice tailed off, his expression anxious.

'And am I worth the difficulties I bring with me?'

Charles nodded.

Unsure how to react, Baggo took some wine. There was an underlying streak of racism in Charles, Cynthia too, but they were trying to overcome it and his own father would approve of everything Charles had just said. He found himself wanting Melanie's father to believe him to be worth the problems he feared. He wanted that very badly.

'I have some time off next week. I planned to revise for my exam but that is going fine so I shall go to St Andrews and help my friend, the inspector. It would be monstrous if your old client's daughter should have both her father and her husband taken from her because of miscarriages of justice. I shall try to make sure that doesn't happen.' He paused. 'Charles.'

Looking surprised, Charles smiled. 'That would be most good of you. Baggo.' He tipped the remaining wine into their glasses and swallowed his in one gulp. 'Perhaps we should join the girls inside. Do you fancy a nightcap?'

When, on their way down the hill, Melanie asked how he had got on with her dad, 'We understand each other,' Baggo said, then told her about his change of plan. She seemed pleased. 'I just wish I could come with you but I'm due in Kilmarnock Sheriff Court on Monday and it's likely to run for three days. Will you cope on your own?' she asked, giving him a playful nudge.

10

It was just after six-thirty and dawn had broken an hour earlier. Flick was changing Verity and planning her day. When she heard her mobile buzz, she groaned. At this time of the morning it would not be good news.

'I'm sorry, ma'am, but there's been another suspicious death,' McKellar told her, 'Jocelyn Montpellier. He was found half an hour ago by a jogger, face down in the Lade Braes burn. Either accident or perhaps murder. I'm on my way now. The constable who responded to the 999 call had the gumption to phone me. I know Montpellier was one of the crowd Cox was with on Friday night.'

Flick immediately wished she had gone to see the Montpelliers the previous evening. She got directions to where the body lay and instructed McKellar to preserve the scene and call SOCOs and Dr MacGregor. 'As it's clear-cut, he can certify death,' she added. 'There's no need to upset Dr Ralston.' Then she thought of someone with whom she wanted to share this moment.

Harriet Cowan grunted as she answered the duty fiscal's phone. Sounding brighter than she felt,

Flick told her about the latest sudden death. Cowan muttered sleepily that she would meet Flick at the scene. Although the fiscal was a pain at the best of times and Flick wished she didn't have to bother with her, disturbing her Sunday morning lie-in made her feel better.

'Poor you,' Fergus said when she woke him to explain, settling the baby in bed beside him. As she dressed he cuddled Verity. 'I'm going to have to work tomorrow,' he told her, 'so I'd better see if Mum can hold the fort.'

'Fine,' she replied, trying to mask her lack of enthusiasm. Mrs Maxwell (Senior) was no fan of working mothers and did not disguise her opinion that Flick did not look after her darling Fergus as well as she should.

'Will your dad come as well?'

'Probably. No show without Punch.'

She sighed. Fergus' father had been a police inspector, and when not reminiscing about 'the old days', tried to offer advice to his son. Fergus put up with this patiently but Flick knew he would be sure to tell her how she should be handling her investigation. Worse, he seldom lost an opportunity to make an anti-English remark. He pretended that these barbs were only jokes but she knew better. A political discussion before the previous year's referendum had degenerated into acrimony. She would have to bite her tongue so long as her in-laws were in the house. They were needed to look after Verity,that was all there was to it, and they adored their only granddaughter. Feeling put-upon, she kissed her husband and Verity then left.

The Lade Braes was a winding, picturesque path running alongside the Kinness Burn from the west to the middle of the town. Lined by tree-covered slopes, it was favoured by dog-walkers and pram-pushers, Flick among them. The body had been found beside the Law Mill Bridge, a hump-backed stone bridge over the burn dating from the eighteenth century. Situated at the west end of the Lade Braes, the Law Mill was a dilapidated, conical building with the skeleton of the mill wheel still visible. Its red pantile roof had holes in it and green moss blocked the gutters. Flick was aware that there had been a mill there for over eight hundred years; like many in-comers, she knew the history of her adopted town better than most native St Andreans. The adjacent bridge led from the main path up through trees to a duck pond which had provided water for the mill. The Mill House, still inhabited, was a short distance downstream from the now neglected mill.

When Flick arrived at the scene, McKellar was directing a young constable who was tying police tape onto the trees round the bridge. He had known Montpellier and confirmed his identity. Paramedics in green overalls stood beside an ambulance parked beside the metal barrier preventing vehicles from the west from going further along the path. Flick found the sight disturbing. This was the point at which she generally turned back towards the town when pushing Verity's pram. Her professional life had impinged on her family life and, she knew irrationally, suddenly felt less safe.

She stood on the bridge and looked down at the body. A tall man, Montpellier was lying on his back just upstream from the bridge, nearly submerged in the burn. His arms were raised, his legs together. He wore black brogues, grey trousers and a navy blue sweater with a white insignia on the left breast. Flick thought she recognised this as the crest of the Royal and Ancient Golf Club. His face was purple. Above his gaping eyes there was a diagonal gash splitting his forehead. Between his head and the bank were a number of large stones with sharp edges, most of them submerged.

'The body was face down and the jogger turned it over. He recognised Mr Montpellier and saw he was dead,' McKellar explained. 'It looks as if he fell from the bridge. Or was pushed,' he added with emphasis.

'Yes,' Flick said. She did not think he had fallen accidentally. She saw that the earth on the bank beside the body had been disturbed. 'Do you think the SOCOs will be able to make anything of that?' she asked, pointing.

'I doubt it, ma'am. There was the jogger and then the paramedics. They had to check he was dead.'

Flick could see damp footprints with traces of mud on the paved surface of the bridge and hoped she was not obliterating important evidence. Standing very still, she inspected the low, moss-covered parapet of the bridge and thought she identified scuff marks, as if someone standing where she was had been pushed from behind, falling head first onto the sharp stones below, their feet being dragged over the low parapet. She would get the SOCOs to check out her theory.

If Montpellier had been pushed, his killer would have wanted to check whether the fall had killed him. They would almost certainly have gone into the water and, if necessary, held his head down until he had drowned. The SOCOs would have to examine the ground and bushes on both banks in case the killer had left some trace. Of course it might have been an accidental trip that caused the fall but with all that had been going on, Flick was almost certain it had been murder.

Her thoughts were interrupted by the arrival of the SOCOs and a photographer, who immediately began to take video shots of the scene. Flick gave her instructions then went to speak to the jogger who had made the grisly discovery.

His name was Martin Silver and she found him, wrapped in a blanket but shivering and clutching his mobile phone, in the passenger seat of the police car parked in front of the ambulance. He was a university lecturer, about thirty and wiry. An ultra-short haircut disguised premature baldness.

'I went out about quarter to six,' he explained, the words coming in a torrent. 'That's my usual time in the summer. I run along the Lade Braes then cross the bridge and sprint up the hill to the duck pond where I do some exercises then turn for home. I was crossing the bridge and about to start sprinting when I saw the body. I had to see if he was dead so I turned him so he was face up. I got a shock – it was a horrible sight. Then I saw it was Mr Montpellier. He had been our family's lawyer but I hadn't seen much of him recently. A few months ago I bumped into him in town and said hello but he just walked past me. His wife was with him. I heard later he had Alzheimer's or dementia. Such a shame. He was a very clever man. When can I go home?'

'Very soon. But please describe exactly how the body lay when you saw it and what you did.'

He grimaced as he thought. 'He was face down, literally. His head was just beside a submerged rock with a sharp edge. It wasn't tilted to either side. His arms were stretched in front of him, but bent at the elbow. His legs were apart. It was almost a star shape, but for the bent arms. I decided to check him and went to the far side of the bridge and through the bushes and down the bank. I pushed his left side so he lay on his back, nearer the middle of the burn. That's when I recognised him.'

Flick was grateful for such a clear account. She thanked him and, as he had given McKellar his contact details, offered him a lift home in a squad car. 'No thank you,' he said. 'This has been a bit of a shock. I think I'd find a run therapeutic.' Flick watched as he jogged along the path towards town, his stride lengthening before he disappeared from view.

'Good morning again, Inspector!' She turned to see Dr MacGregor coming down the path towards her from the direction of the main road. As well as the usual silk bow tie he wore olive green fisherman's waders that came up to his crotch and made him walk awkwardly. He looked like a prat, in Flick's opinion. 'I parked on the main road to prevent getting blocked in,' he explained. 'I am due to read the lesson in church so I can't spend too long here.'

She smiled apologetically. 'I'm sorry to bother you again, but I suspect your evidence will be very important: cause of death, time of death and whether it was accident or murder. Or even suicide. Oh, and you'll need to certify that he's dead. There seemed no point in calling Dr Ralston just to state the obvious.'

'Well let's get on with it. You will see I come prepared for an aquatic investigation.'

She saw how he greeted the SOCOs by name, joking about the St Andrews murder rate, then stood on the bridge looking down at his latest customer. She marvelled at how he could carry off his ridiculous attire with such confidence and supposed it had something to do with an expensive education. Plus the fact that he was the best, and knew it.

Flick watched MacGregor going about his business, first in the water then on the bridge, after the paramedics had lifted the body from the burn and laid it out for him in an open body-bag. She was unaware of Harriet Cowan's approach.

'I hope this isn't a waste of time,' Cowan snapped.

Flick turned and caught a waft of peppermint off her breath. The fiscal's eyes were bloodshot and she shivered under a voluminous sweater although it was not a cold morning. Flick updated her succinctly but wondered how much she was taking in; she seemed distracted. 'Good night, last night?' Flick asked.

Cowan moved away. 'Nothing special. I don't do early mornings.'

At this point MacGregor came over, puffing at a newly-lit cigar. Cowan winced when the smoke hit her nostrils and the pathologist smiled. 'I've done what I can here and all I can say with confidence is that he died a few hours ago, probably a bit before midnight. For a more exact time and the cause of death you'll have to wait till after the post mortem tomorrow. He's second in the queue. Now I'll be on my way.'

'We're very grateful to you, doctor,' Flick said. 'That's two consecutive early morning call-outs,' she added for Cowan's benefit.

'"To whomever much is given, of him much will be required; and to whom much was entrusted, of him more will be asked." – Luke 12. Something to bear in mind. I shall read it with gusto later this morning.' With a wave, and with waders flapping, he set off up the slope towards his car.

'Well there's not much for me to do here, so I'll await your report tomorrow morning,' the fiscal said.

'Do you have someone waiting for you on the main road? If not, I think you should allow me to get a constable to drive you home,' Flick said.

'My car's up there,' she replied defensively, taking care not to breathe in Flick's direction.

'And I really think it should stay there,' Flick said firmly.

'All right,' Cowan agreed huffily.

Relishing a moral victory, Flick organised a car for the fiscal then found out from McKellar where Montpellier had lived. It was close by. Taking him with her, she set off on foot to inform the next of kin one more time. She didn't look forward to it.

11

A gleaming Mercedes, a battered Fiat and the spotless, white Golf Flick had seen in the Lightbodys' driveway were parked on the gravel in front of the Montpelliers' home. It was an upset-looking James Lightbody who answered the doorbell, his assertiveness of the previous day absent.

'Oh, good morning, Inspector. You'll be here about Joss. Do come in.' As Flick and McKellar entered the hall, Lightbody whispered, 'Georgia knows about Joss. Edna Silver lives round the corner and her son found him on his morning jog. Edna came round to break the news.'

He led the way into the sitting room, which was situated at the front of the house. Red walls were decorated with so many paintings that the room resembled an art gallery with no coherent theme. Flick identified a Bellany, a wide-eyed, delicate woman, next to a staring man with bulging muscles by Howson. There were abstracts and Art Deco, nothing bland.

There were six people in the room. All looked miserable. Norma Lightbody sat on an upright chair, dabbing her eyes with a handkerchief. A man with a highly-coloured face and a swollen nose sat squashed on a sofa between two women, one younger than the rest. Beside them a large, comfortable-looking armchair was empty. On a second sofa a bald man sat beside a woman who turned a tear-stained face towards Flick. Her make-up was smudged and her jet-black hair was in disarray, lacquer making it stick out in odd directions. She wore creased red trousers and a blue shirt. A black pashmina wrapped round her shoulders didn't stop her shivering. 'I've heard, Inspector,' she said, her voice catching, after Flick had introduced herself.

'I'm very sorry, Mrs Montpellier,' Flick said, unsure about how she should play the situation.

'I'm afraid there's no doubt it's your husband,' McKellar said.

The woman nodded.

'He was found face-down in the Lade Braes burn,' Flick said. 'It would be helpful to know how he came to be there.'

The man with the swollen nose looked indignant. 'Can this not wait, Inspector? Mrs Montpellier has had a terrible shock.' His diction was distorted by his blocked nose, his clothes were crumpled and he needed a shave.

'It's all right, Kevin. The inspector has her job to do.' The widow sat up and stuck her chin out. 'Last night after dinner I sat in here to watch television. My husband went to his study to play his favourite CDs. He has, had, dementia and it's been getting worse. We normally go to bed about eleven. When I went through to get him, I found the CD was finished and he wasn't there. He sometimes goes walkabout, but never before at night. He must have gone out without me noticing. Of course the curtains in this room were closed. I checked he wasn't in the house or garden then I phoned the JBs. There's a group of us, we've been friends for ages.' She looked round at the others. 'Anyway they looked for Joss but couldn't find him.' She paused, collecting herself. 'I also phoned Police Scotland on101. The person on the switchboard told me your patrols would keep an eye out but it wasn't an emergency.' She sniffed. 'It was a mild night and I thought he must have just settled himself somewhere and gone to sleep. I didn't go to bed. Kevin stayed with me in case he could help. Then Edna Silver came round, breaking the news.' She gulped.

'I phoned the rest. We all want to be here for Georgia,' Kevin McPhail added.

'How did he die? Did he suffer?' Georgia Montpellier asked hesitantly, close to tears.

'I can't say now. We'll know more after the post mortem tomorrow. I'm afraid that will be necessary,' Flick added, seeing the distress on the widow's face. 'Now please would you all identify yourselves.' As they did so she searched their faces. If Montpellier had been murdered, these were the prime suspects. Maybe one of them had killed Cox as well. But they all gave the appearance of being ordinary, decent people, understandably upset by a sudden death. She would need to obtain full statements from all of them individually.

Leaving McKellar in the sitting room, Flick phoned Di Falco then Detective Sergeant Lance Wallace, who had been due to return from holiday in Spain the previous evening. He was not expected back on duty until the Monday but Flick needed his calm, methodical back-up. His gruff, reassuring voice contained no hint of resentment as he agreed to meet her at the Montpelliers' house in half an hour.

Returning to the sitting room, Flick said, 'As this is a sudden, unexplained death it will be necessary to investigate it. The procurator fiscal is quite likely to order a Fatal Accident Inquiry. I will need to obtain statements from you all individually. Two more officers will be arriving shortly to assist. I regret the inconvenience, but we should be finished in a couple of hours or so. Please stay here with PC McKellar. First, Mrs Montpellier, might we go to another room, perhaps your husband's study, you said he had one?'

She nodded and led Flick through the uncluttered hall, past a door with a paper label, TOILET, stuck on with sellotape just above her eye level, to a room at the back of the house. It was dominated by a grand, brown wood desk with a flat surface of scuffed, dark green leather. It was almost certainly a genuine antique, Flick thought. A laptop and a telephone had both been pushed to the far side. The most striking item was a photograph in which a tall, dark-haired young man in an academic gown stood between his proud parents, the Bodleian Library prominent in the background. His elegant, assured mother was almost unrecognisable as the woman Flick was about to interview.

The desk looked out through French doors to the garden. There was a key in the lock of the French doors, both of which had a label reading GLASS stuck to them. A more modern swivel chair was in front of the desk and on a low table beside it sat a music system and a rack of CDs. A box set of *Carmen* lay on top of the rack. Two walls were lined with bookshelves containing an eclectic collection of literary classics, biographies, golf books and modern fiction. On one shelf, a few well-used legal textbooks were outnumbered by Rumpole paperbacks. The shelf below held several Flashman books. Flick, who had a degree in English Literature, noted many paperbacks by Agatha Christie and Dorothy L Sayers, Ian Rankin and Val McDermid. Crime fiction paperbacks by lesser-known authors filled one of the bottom shelves. There were two armchairs, stains on the arms of both suggesting steady wear over a long period. In a corner an old-fashioned wooden butter churn contained several golf clubs, most with wooden shafts. The wall to the right of the door was filled with golfing prints. In pride of place was a photograph of a younger, fleshier Montpellier shaking hands with Arnold Palmer. Just by looking round the room, Flick was forming a picture of the dead man before he'd been enfeebled by dementia.

'We both love crime fiction,' Georgia Montpellier said, noting Flick's interest in the bookshelves. The remark was mundane but the catch in her voice betrayed her emotional state.

'May I?' Flick asked as she opened the music system and examined the CD, Act 1 of *Carmen*. 'How long does this take to play?'

Georgia Montpellier shrugged. 'Nearly an hour, I suppose. Doesn't it say?'

'No it doesn't,' Flick said, sliding the CD back in then sitting in the swivel chair at the desk and bringing out her notebook and pen. 'Now, if you feel able, I'd be grateful if you could take me slowly through the events of yesterday evening.'

Georgia sat on the edge of one of the armchairs, her hands between her knees. A pained look made Flick think she was about to break down but she held herself together, not saying anything until she was ready. The room faced north-east but a ray of sunlight hit the wall beside the French doors, lightening the room and making the smudging of Georgia's make-up, particularly the painted eyebrows, grotesquely obvious. The woman was shattered, effectively deconstructed, if that was the right word. This would be the time to get her to reveal herself.

'We had our dinner about eight ...'

'What did you have?'

'Roast chicken. Joss' favourite.' She sniffed. 'Bread

sauce and oatmeal stuffing, spinach and new potatoes. Then cranachan.'

'What's that?'

'Oatmeal, honey and raspberries in whipped cream. I tried to give Joss a special dinner on Saturdays. It was good for him to taste things he'd always enjoyed. I opened a bottle of Chateau Batailley he'd laid down before ... I could close my eyes and imagine ... But you can't turn the clock back,' she added briskly, wiping a tear.

'When did you finish eating?'

'I don't know. Half past eight, quarter to nine perhaps. Why?'

'We need to try to fix the time of death,' Flick said softly.

'Of course, yes.'

Another silence followed, Georgia gulping, keeping herself under control.

'After dinner?' Flick prompted.

'I washed up then watched a DVD of *House of Cards* in the sitting room. Kevin Spacey, you know. I loved it, but Joss couldn't follow it. He couldn't follow most things, actually. Most evenings after dinner, I'd watch TV in the sitting room and he'd play his CDs in his study. He'd play the same one over and over again. I was sick of hearing Act 1 of *Carmen*. But it gave him pleasure so ... Anyway I watched two episodes of *House of Cards*, each lasting a bit less than an hour. When I went to get him up to bed the CD was finished and he wasn't there.'

'And the time?'

'Just before eleven. Maybe ten, five to.'

'And you hadn't seen or heard anything out of the ordinary?'

'No. The sitting room curtains were shut and I didn't hear a door or anything. He had just disappeared. I wondered if he had gone to bed but he hadn't. I searched the house then the garden. Then I phoned our friends.'

'Were the curtains here in the study closed?'

'No. He never bothered with them.'

'And the key to the French doors, was it in the lock?'

'Yes. And the door was shut but unlocked. It should have been locked. I haven't touched anything. We normally kept the key there during spells of fine weather.'

'Would your friends have known that?'

'I suppose so, but you can't think any of them … None of them would harm Joss. They all respected him. Loved him, yes, loved him. He'd been the leader of the pack when he was himself.'

'Dementia's terribly cruel,' Flick said. 'It must be awful when someone close to you acts inappropriately because their brain's not functioning properly.'

The hint of a smile crossed Georgia's face. 'Thank you, yes. Joss could be very silly.'

'You'll know we're investigating Eric Cox's murder. I hear last night at dinner in the Adamson your husband said and did some strange things, pretending to shoot Mr McPhail?'

She shook her head. 'He started teasing Kevin McPhail about an incident years ago. Our son David and Kevin's son Keith were friends. The McPhails lived in Lawhead Road East at the time and the bottoms of our gardens were close. It was bonfire night and David was home from Glenalmond for the weekend. He and Keith started firing rockets at each other's houses. They even threw fireworks at each other. Joss could see how dangerous it was but Kevin, who'd had a few drinks, thought it was fun and let off a couple of rockets himself. One of the McPhails' neighbours called the police. Joss had to do a lot of smooth talking to persuade them not to prosecute. Kevin's always been sensitive about it, but last night Joss went on and on. I couldn't stop him and I could see Kevin was annoyed.'

'This computer, did he still use it?' Flick pointed to the laptop on the desk.

'No. He couldn't remember the password to get into it and I didn't know it. I have my own computer upstairs. I wanted to take this one away but he said he'd remember the password one day. Of course he never did. It was the same with books. He hasn't read one for over a year but he liked everything to stay the same. He would sit in this chair for hours, his mouth open, playing CDs, mostly operas, the same one over and over again.'

'I'd like to take the computer. It probably won't tell us anything, but you never know.'

Georgia shrugged. 'If you want.'

'Did he have a mobile phone?'

'Yes. I tried to make him carry it with him in case he went walkabout or got lost. He didn't have it with him last night. It's in the top drawer of the desk. I suppose you'll want to take it too.'

'Yes please.' Flick swung round and took an unsophisticated mobile from the drawer. Beside it were a number of yellow post-it notes: 'Turandot', 'Jimmy L', 'brush teeth' and many more written in a spidery hand. 'I'd like to take these as well,' Flick said. Georgia nodded.

'Did he get depressed?' Flick asked.

It took a moment for Georgia to answer. 'Frustrated, more like. He sometimes went into terrible rages. They were very hard to take. He'd always been so equable. If ever he lashed out it was with his tongue. But there have been times recently … I felt scared of him.' She buried her face in her hands and wept. 'I loved him still but he was leaving me, bit by bit, day by day,' she sobbed. 'We still had times when there was some point to everything and they were precious. I'm not ready to lose him, I'm not. This is a nightmare. Sorry.' She sat breathing deeply, making every effort to collect herself. Flick didn't doubt that her grief was genuine.

'You say he went walkabout?' she asked gently.

'From time to time he'd wander out, generally into town. Someone usually took him in and phoned me. Sometimes I managed to cut him off at the pass.' She smiled wryly.

'Had he ever gone to the Lade Braes?'

'Once or twice. He'd been taken there as a small boy. I think he would have used the footpath across the road from the house.'

'But he hadn't done this at night?'

'No.'

'It would have been getting dark soon after you finished your dinner?'

'Yes. I don't understand it. But I suppose that's dementia.'

'Did you hear his music after you began to watch the TV, for example between episodes of *House of Cards*?'

'Yes. I went to the loo between episodes and the same CD was playing, but I didn't go to see him. That would have been about ten.'

'Would you have heard if he had left by the front door?'

'Probably. There's a glass door inside as well as the front door itself. They both make a bit of a noise. They were both shut.'

'So when you hadn't found him in the house or garden, you phoned your friends. What time was that?'

'Just after eleven.'

'And they were all at home?'

'Yes. I phoned the house numbers, Kevin McPhail first then Jimmy Lightbody then Hugh Harkins. They all helped. Kevin looked along the Lade Braes. He went on foot from the west end of the walk, shouting

Joss' name. But it was dark and he didn't go far along. He came back and stayed with me. Jimmy drove round the nearby streets and Hugh drove round town with Susan. Eventually they gave up. Kevin stayed the night here in case he was needed. I didn't go to bed, as you can probably see.'

'After Mrs Silver brought the news, has anyone contacted your son?' Flick nodded towards the photograph on the desk.

'Kevin took care of that. David's a financial analyst in London. He'll be flying up today.'

'Is there anyone else who should be informed?'

'No one close. Kevin said he would help with all that.'

'Did your husband have any enemies who might want to hurt him?'

Georgia looked shocked. 'I really can't think of anyone who'd want to kill him. Do you think he was murdered?'

'We're keeping open minds. This investigation has to be thorough.'

Georgia nodded. 'I suppose so.'

'Lastly, did anything unusual happen recently but yesterday in particular, anything at all, whether you think it might be relevant or not?'

Georgia thought for a moment. 'There was a horrible journalist who came here just before dinner last night. He talked to Joss, who was outside practising his pitching. I sent him packing. He went to see Kevin McPhail and assaulted him. He was asking questions about that murderer, Peter Waldron, who's been released. Kevin phoned you, the police. I think the journalist may have given his name but I can't remember it if he did.'

'What did he look like?' Flick wanted to find this man.

'Fat, red-faced, badly dressed. Spoke with a cockney accent.'

Flick immediately thought of her old nemesis Inspector No, but this couldn't be him. He was in Andalucia, spending his ill-deserved pension on cheap Spanish wine and easy Spanish women. The journalist Georgia had described would stick out like a sore thumb in St Andrews. It would not be hard to trace him. She thanked Georgia, who looked relieved as they returned to the sitting room. In the hall Di Falco and a sun-tanned Wallace awaited instructions.

* * *

As Georgia went upstairs to lie down, Flick went outside with Di Falco and Wallace. They walked a short distance down the drive, away from Hugh Harkins who was puffing nervously at a cigarette. Di Falco had already explained the background to the sergeant and it did not take long for Flick to tell them what she was particularly interested in. While she would interview both Harkins in the study, Di Falco would see the Lightbodys in the kitchen and Wallace would speak to the McPhails in another room.

Hugh Harkins was one of those people who could not help looking guilty, Flick thought. He sat on the edge of the same chair Georgia had sat on, his left shoulder twitching, occasionally scratching his bald head as he confirmed that he and Susan had been at home when Georgia had phoned the house phone about eleven. They had got into their car and driven round the streets of the town, looking for Joss. It had been busy because of the Lammas Market, but Joss would have stood out on account of his height. They had stayed in touch with the others by mobile and gone out to the Montpelliers' about midnight. They hadn't stayed long. Kevin McPhail and Jimmy Lightbody had been there. Kevin had volunteered to stay the night with Georgia. They had gone home but when Kevin had phoned with the bad news, had returned to the Montpelliers'.

Flick asked what they had done earlier.

'We had been at the McPhails' for dinner. The evening was spoiled by a journalist who sneaked up on us then pestered us with questions about Peter Waldron. He actually assaulted Mr McPhail. The police were called and I believe they caught the man nearby. Mr McPhail was asked to identify him sitting in the back of a squad car. But the evening was ruined. Mr McPhail cleaned himself up and changed his shirt then we ate quickly and left.'

'When was that?'

'About quarter to ten.'

'How did you get back?'

'By car. I drove. We had a cup of tea when we got home and watched television until Georgia phoned just after eleven.'

'Do you know the journalist's name?'

'No. He was a nasty piece of work. And a slob.'

'The previous evening, I understand your group had dinner at the Adamson?'

'Correct.'

'And did Mr Montpellier annoy Mr McPhail in some way?'

'I gather so. I was at the other end of the table so I didn't hear what was going on. Mr Montpellier was pointing at Mr McPhail, but I was talking to Mr Lightbody, who was opposite me.'

'And did you go to play golf in the dark after dinner?'

'You've heard about that? Yes. We shouldn't have, I know.' By now his shoulder twitch was working overtime.

'And Mr Montpellier was with you?'

'Yes. He was a fine player in his day. He still has, had a lovely swing. In the last year or so he often forgot where he had just hit the ball, but on Friday night in the dark it was difficult for all of us to see where our balls had gone. He could remember the course though. He'd played it so often as a young man.'

'Did he talk much with Mr Cox?'

'With Mr Cox?'

'Yes, the man who was murdered in the early hours of Saturday.'

'I don't know. I was too busy trying to find my own ball. They both got into Cottage Bunker on the fourth, I remember that.' Harkins was giving every appearance of cooperating, albeit nervously.

'I believe your wife called off the dinner at the Adamson?'

'Yes. She made an excuse but frankly she didn't want to meet Mary Spencer. There was a bit of history there.'

'Do you think Mrs Spencer blamed her for what happened to her husband?'

'She may have done, for all I know. Susan preferred to avoid her if possible.'

'But after dinner the women went back to your flat on The Scores?'

'Linda McPhail suggested the ladies should check on Susan while we played golf. I said yes and gave her the keys of the flat. I thought Susan might be in bed but she wasn't. I gather Mary Spencer left quite soon, certainly before we returned from the golf.'

'When did the party break up?'

'Twenty, quarter to two roughly.'

'In what order did they leave?

'I'd given everyone a dram. Mr Montpellier was tired and Georgia took him home. Mr Cox got up as they left. The McPhails and the Lightbodys left with him. Susan went to bed and I cleared up.'

'How did the McPhails get home?'

He looked at his feet. 'Mr McPhail drove. I know he shouldn't have. He offered the Lightbodys a lift but Norma wanted to walk.'

'Do you know anyone who might have wanted Mr Montpellier dead?'

He looked appalled. 'Surely it must have been some sort of accident? But no, there would be no reason to kill him.'

'Then were you aware of any bouts of depression that might have led him to take his own life?'

He screwed up his face then shook his head. 'His condition got him down, I know, but Georgia looked after him so well … We did our best to include him in things. He was always very gregarious. He enjoyed the company even if he didn't follow what was said. In his prime, he'd have hated to see himself as he was latterly, but you could tell that, for all the frustration, in his own estimation he still had something to live for.'

Flick changed tack. 'I gather you went to Cupar police office to see Cameron Smith yesterday morning?'

'Yes but I don't want to talk about that.'

'But I gather he has another lawyer.'

'It's too early to say. The situation's a bit confused.'

'Very well, but can you tell us anything that might shed some light on either of these two sudden deaths within twenty-four hours, both of which have a connection to your JB group?'

Harkins looked startled, as if he'd not thought of it in that way. 'No, Inspector. I can't' His shoulder twitched violently.

Flick looked at him appraisingly. Despite his

guilty manner he had seemed to answer frankly and openly. But he had told her nothing of substance she did not already know. It was time to speak to his wife.

Susan Harkins, formerly Susan Waldron, was as assured as her husband was unsettled. She gave Flick a condescending smile as she took her seat elegantly in the armchair her husband had not occupied then took a cigarette packet and lighter from her handbag. She lit up and exhaled, not at Flick but so that smoke would drift in her direction. 'So many places don't supply ashtrays these days,' she said, placing a small brass box open on the arm of her chair. 'How can I help you?'

The way she pronounced 'I' as 'Ei' told Flick that her upper-class accent was affected. She noted the dark trouser suit and the carefully-applied make-up. There was not a hair out of place. The gardener's short nails and rough hands provided the sole discordant note, although the eye was drawn to ostentatiously jewelled rings. Flick suspected they were fake.

'I would like to know what you can tell me about the events of last night.'

'There's not much I can say.'

That was true. Her account, delivered with a weary arrogance, matched her husband's. It was the same with the previous night. She knew of no one who might have wanted to harm Montpellier and she was sure he hadn't committed suicide; it must have been a tragic accident. Flick's instincts told her that something was being kept from her.

'How did the Jolly Boys come into being?' she asked.

Susan Harkins looked at her disdainfully. 'What has that got to do with these inquiries?'

'Maybe nothing, maybe quite a lot. That will be for me to judge.'

'Well it's no secret. It started at Edinburgh University. There was my first husband, Peter Waldron, Jimmy Lightbody, Tony Spencer and Joss. They were all doing Law, they all played rugby and came from Fife. Joss was the leader. Law was his second degree; he'd been at Oxford. He was so intelligent then. And very, very charming.' Tilting her head back, she looked down her nose at Flick as if to say, 'You wouldn't know such persons.'

Flick thought, 'I bet you fancied him and had to settle for second best.' She said, 'So I've heard.'

The would-be *grande dame* continued, 'They got up to the sort of nonsense students get up to. I was doing Social Sciences and went around with them sometimes. They were joined in their last year by Kevin McPhail. They called him "the kid" but he doesn't like to be reminded of that. He came from Fife as well. After university they all came back to Fife. Joss, Jimmy, Peter and Tony all joined different firms of solicitors. Kevin started a property company. Hugh, my present husband, was in the same firm of solicitors as my first husband. They got on well and he became a Jolly Boy too. The group has stuck together despite all the ups and downs.'

There was no hint of embarrassment or hesitation about this account. 'I understand you had an affair with Tony Spencer?' Flick asked sharply.

A slight raising of an eyebrow was the only facial reaction. It occurred to Flick that her unwrinkled skin might owe much to Botox. 'Yes. These things happen in life. You'll know that, Inspector?'

Flick ignored the question. 'And that affair led to Tony Spencer being murdered?'

'My first husband was a jealous man.'

'And your second husband stepped into his shoes, with you and the firm?'

Susan stared, her cold eyes and long eyelashes accentuated by her thick, frameless glasses. 'I don't care for your tone, Inspector. I've told you all you could possibly need to know.' She rose and walked out.

Flick stopped herself from calling her back. She couldn't force her to speak and she didn't want to needlessly antagonise this tight-knit group. She waited in the hall until Di Falco and Wallace had finished, then gave the computer, mobile and notes to Di Falco with instructions to take them to Cupar where DC Spider Gilsland, a techy expert, would examine them. 'We'll have a briefing at noon,' she said. 'Any ideas about these deaths will be welcome.'

It was just after ten and she was exhausted. Why had she not become a teacher? If she had worked at all on a Sunday morning it would have been marking essays while her daughter played and her husband was on the golf course. But she would not have met Fergus; it would be a different husband, a different child … She wouldn't change things, even if she could. She drove home. An hour with them would be worthwhile. On the way her mobile buzzed. It was a text from Baggo: 'I'm coming to help you'.

12

Baggo drove his second-hand Golf across Fife wired with nervous excitement. This was his chance to really impress Melanie's father. Never before had he wanted to settle down with a girl. There had been plenty in the past but no one had ticked all the boxes that she did. It was far more than that, though. She gave him butterflies in his stomach. A poet would say she made his heart leap. He snorted; that was sentimental rubbish. But the fact remained that he was deeply in love.

That morning they had made love, had scrambled eggs, toast and coffee in bed, then made love again. Showered, shaved and satisfied, he felt up for the challenge ahead. He looked forward to seeing Flick Fortune again. In their early days in Wimbledon CID she had been his sergeant. He'd made a half-hearted pass at her which she had ignored. Thank goodness because, despite their differences, they were now friends as well as colleagues who worked well together. She really was colour-blind; she saw him as a human being, not as an Indian. That was more than could be said for many people as politically correct as she was, who talked the talk but didn't walk the walk. She was thawing too, no longer an iron-knickers woman;

there had even been hints of a real sense of humour, though he still enjoyed teasing her.

He arrived in Cupar early for the twelve o' clock briefing to be greeted by Sergeant Lance Wallace, another old friend.

'Baggo! What on earth are you doing here?'

'Lancelot! I am here to help you with your murdered political activist.' It was said that Lance had been conceived after his parents had seen *Camelot* and Baggo was not going to let him forget it.

'Well there's been another suspicious death and it looks as if they may be related.' Lance brought Baggo up to date with the latest developments.

'So the plot thickens,' he commented. 'I see you have been exposing yourself to the sun. You're a lot browner than I am.' Baggo could not understand the preoccupation with tanning of many blessed with white skin.

'We're just back from a fortnight in Spain, an apartment in Estepona.'

'Just you and Jeannie?'

'All four of us. Students can't resist a free holiday.'

'The Bank of Dad is a most popular institution.'

'Aye. This overtime will be welcome.'

From another part of the building angry shouts could be heard.

'Another unhappy customer?' Baggo asked.

'Someone the inspector won't be pleased to see. A man posing as a journalist assaulted one of these so-called Jolly Boys. He was arrested last night and it turns out he's the Inspector No from your Wimbledon days. Goodness knows what he's doing here. He's demanding to see the inspector, whom he calls Felicity. He says he taught her everything she knows. Do you remember the last time he stuck his nose into an investigation?'

'Too well.' Osborne had been a thorn in their flesh, making scathing comments in the press about the inquiry.

'Do you want to see him?'

'No. He can stew in his own juice till after the briefing. Flick should call the shots.'

'Anyway, have you been seconded to help?'

'No. I'm here unofficially. I'm supposed to be studying for my inspector's exam. But I think I'm OK. Flick and Billy Di Falco visited me yesterday when they were informing the next of kin and told me about the case. I have reason to believe that Waldron may have been wrongly convicted back in 1984, so there may be something to put right and it may have a bearing on your inquiry.'

'Right.' Lance saw complications – and overtime.

Baggo was about to criticise the milky, tasteless coffee he was given when Flick arrived. She asked him to come to her office. He told her what Melanie's father had said about Waldron's case; he hoped he might unofficially assist the investigation.

Flick said nothing at first and Baggo feared he was going to be sent home with his tail between his legs. 'I'm grateful, of course I am,' she said hesitantly, 'but this is going to be high-profile and I'll be blamed if something goes wrong. Stay in the background and no maverick stunts. None,' she added forcefully in response to his expression of injured innocence.

He wanted to remind her of the successes they had both enjoyed as a result of his maverick stunts but bit his tongue. 'I will behave myself,' he said humbly. She wished she could believe him.

When the briefing started she welcomed Baggo to the team, emphasising his unofficial role. 'I don't want his fingerprints on any important aspects of the inquiry. He will be a great help, I'm sure, but he is to be kept in the background.'

She carried on, 'Dr MacGregor will phone me with his findings after the post mortems tomorrow. They will be particularly important in relation to Montpellier's case. At the moment it could be accident, suicide or murder, but until we learn otherwise I think we should assume it was murder. The SOCOs tell me there were signs of activity on the bank of the burn nearest the body but they couldn't get any worthwhile evidence; the jogger who found the body and the paramedics had gone into the water to check the body. They did find scuff marks on the low parapet of the bridge, suggesting that he had fallen forward, dragging his feet behind him.' Turning to DC Spider Gilsland, she asked if he had made any progress with Montpellier's phone or computer.

Looking unusually smart in a short-sleeved shirt that had been ironed and chinos not bearing evidence of his recent feeding habits, Gilsland cleared his throat. 'The phone hadn't been used for five weeks and the computer hadn't been used for twenty-two months. I couldn't find anything relevant on either of them, but I've only had a quick check. Do you want me to keep digging, ma'am? And if so, what am I looking for?'

Flick said, 'Thank you Spider, but right now I can't see the point. It's good to see you so smart,' she added. She had ticked him off for scruffiness on many occasions.

He blushed. 'Spider's in love,' his close friend Di Falco said in a stage whisper. The others smiled and the blush intensified.

'Jocelyn Montpellier's body was found in the burn beside the Law Mill Bridge,' Flick said, frowning at Di Falco. 'There are two routes there from his house.' She went to the whiteboard and drew an isosceles triangle lying on one side. 'The house is the last one on the right of Hepburn Gardens as you leave St Andrews, just short of the junction with Lawhead Road East. The road continues westwards, downhill. About three hundred yards on the left is the west end of the Lade Braes path. It's just wide enough to take a vehicle at that point but about a hundred and fifty yards down from the junction there's a metal barrier. Beyond the barrier the path divides. You can either turn right over the bridge or continue straight ahead towards town. If Montpellier took that route he would have turned right on leaving his house, continued down the road then turned left on to the Lade Braes, down to the barrier and then right on to the bridge.

'The other route is more direct.' She pointed to the narrow base of the isosceles triangle. 'Diagonally opposite his house is a narrow, unpaved path which descends steeply to the Lade Braes and meets the main path roughly opposite the Mill House. On the left as you go down are garden walls, on the right there's a wood. If he went that way, at the bottom he would have turned right along the Lade Braes until he turned left on to the bridge. His wife told me he'd gone off on his own a couple of times and probably used that route.' She looked round to check that everyone followed her. 'I asked the SOCOs to check the narrow path and they found nothing useful. With the dry weather the path didn't show footprints. So we don't know which route he took.'

'Why do you assume it's murder, ma'am?' McKellar asked. 'He had gone off on his own before.'

'But not at night, and less than twenty-four hours after Cox was definitely murdered. It's too much of a coincidence for me.'

'It's going to be hard to prove,' Lance Wallace said.

Gilsland said, 'An uncle of mine had dementia. It was like the hard drive of a computer with a virus, bit by bit his mind stopped working. Sometimes he hallucinated. Mr Montpellier might have wandered off, thinking God knows what. Maybe he thought he was diving into deep water.'

'Or maybe he had just had enough and decided to end it all,' McKellar said.

'You're right,' Flick said, 'Anything is possible. We're not dealing with a rational man. My feeling is that the most likely scenario is that someone he knew came to the French doors. He let them in and they led him off and pushed him off the bridge then checked he was dead.'

'That would be one of the Jolly Boys or one of their wives,' Di Falco said.

'But why?' Wallace asked.

'To prevent him from talking about something. He was quite disinhibited,' Di Falco said.

'Almost certainly,' Flick agreed. She summarised what Georgia Montpellier and the Harkins had told her.

'I remember the fireworks incident,' Wallace said when she finished. 'I'd recently arrived in this area and was in uniform. The neighbour was furious, rightly. I got both boys down to the station and tore a strip off them, showed them a cell, explained the damage fireworks can do. I think they learned their lesson. I gave McPhail a bollocking too but he was an arrogant sod.'

'What did the McPhails have to say for themselves, Lance?' Flick asked.

'Last night they were having a drink with the Harkins on their patio when someone who said he was a journalist surprised them. He was asking questions about the Peter Waldron case back in 1984 then launched an unprovoked attack on Kevin McPhail. They called the police and the man's in custody but the evening was ruined. The Harkins left early, about quarter to ten. Georgia Montpellier phoned them at about eleven. McPhail left his wife at home and went by car to the Montpelliers. He went down to the Lade Braes using the path opposite the house. He shouted for Montpellier but got no answer. It was dark and he couldn't see so he gave up before he got to the bridge. You know the rest. Linda McPhail said the same as her husband in every detail. She drove here this morning when they heard the news.'

Flick said, 'I'd like to know what the journalist can tell us. Lance, you talk to him after the briefing.'

'Right ma'am.' He shook his head at Baggo. The shouting from the cell, plainly audible in the foyer, could not be heard in the briefing room.

'What did the McPhails say about the previous evening?' Flick asked.

'They were both quite open about the golf. They had the party at the Harkins' flat breaking up at twenty or quarter to two, the same as the Harkins, and people leaving in the same order: the Montpelliers, Cox then the Lightbodys, who walked, and the McPhails. Kevin McPhail admitted he drove though he shouldn't have.'

Flick asked, 'Did he say anything about what Montpellier did to irritate him in the restaurant?'

'He came out with the fireworks story. I don't think he recognised me as the policeman who gave him a bollocking. I would have thought someone like McPhail would have laughed it off, but he claims Montpellier went on and on about it and he got irritated.'

'McPhail is the one with the property company?' Baggo asked.

Flick agreed.

'And that was the case in 1984?'

'Yes.'

He frowned thoughtfully.

'What about the Lightbodys?' Flick turned to Di Falco.

'Mary Spencer arrived in a taxi. After their lasagne James Lightbody gave her a lift to her B and B about ten. He was at pains to say he hadn't been drinking, having had a lot the previous night. When he got home his wife was in bed. He did the washing-up then watched TV and was about to go to bed when Georgia phoned just after eleven. He drove round the streets at this end of town but found nothing.'

Flick wrote the names on the whiteboard. 'So the stories match. Alex, did you see any evidence of collusion when they were left in the sitting room with you?'

'No ma'am. Either they're all telling the truth or they were ready for us.'

Flick said, 'The thing that may not stack up is what Montpellier said to annoy McPhail in the Adamson. Remind me, Billy, what did the waiter say?'

'Amanda.' Di Falco found the page of his notebook. 'Yes, Montpellier pointed to himself then McPhail going "pow, pow" as if shooting. His wife told him to be quiet. Later, Montpellier said to McPhail, "We pulled you out of the shit and no one lost in the end." Something like that. McPhail was really angry.'

'And remember Norma Lightbody said Czechoslovakia was mentioned and her husband changed the subject?' Flick said. 'It doesn't fit with the fireworks story.'

'Czechoslovakia?' Baggo asked.

'Yes,' Flick replied.

'Maybe it was Czechs. Or cheques.' Ignoring the puzzled looks he continued, 'And in 1984 the Jolly Boys were all local solicitors except McPhail, who had a property company?'

'Yes. Why?' Flick asked impatiently.

Baggo nodded his head and smiled. 'In the early 1980s there was a big case in Edinburgh. They still talk about it in the Fraud Squad. It was called the Whitehill Properties case. There was this property company, Whitehill Properties, that specialised in the cheaper end of the market. They used two or three firms of solicitors, pushing buyers and sellers towards these firms too. The business was very lucrative for the lawyers, money for old rope. When the property company ran into difficulties and the bank was reluctant to extend its overdraft the solicitors tried to help it. They started cross-firing cheques. You see, at that time almost all transactions were done by cheque and it took a few days for cheques to clear. When assessing a business, banks looked at cleared funds only, not at cheques that might bounce. Certain cheques were privileged and regarded as cleared as soon as they were lodged. Because of the regulation of their profession, solicitors' cheques were privileged; the risk of them being dishonoured was minimal.

'So cross-firing worked this way. On Monday morning the solicitor and the property company would exchange cheques for, say, ten thousand pounds. That day the company would lodge the solicitor's cheque with their bank, which would immediately regard it as cleared and the company would get the benefit of it. But by the time the company's cheque had been lodged with the solicitor's bank and gone through the clearing system, it could be the end of the week before the ten thousand pounds was debited from the company's account. Many such transactions had two effects. One, they gave a false impression of the company's liquidity. Two, they gave a false impression of the amount of business the company was doing. Of course it had to be done cleverly and not too obviously. In Whitehill Properties they opened files for clients and properties that did not exist. And they would have got off with it if the business had survived, but it crashed and the bank lost a lot of money. Even then it took many months of painstaking work to see what had been going on. A solicitor went to jail.

'I think there was cross-firing here. It fits with what was said in the restaurant and McPhail's anger at Montpellier. It would have led the bank to give the company more leeway than they otherwise would have done. It was highly illegal and if those responsible had been caught they would have gone to jail. But as the company survived it was never discovered. I believe Spencer's murder had something to do with it, and the real killer successfully framed Waldron. As Montpellier became disinhibited, losing his short-term memory but remembering stuff that happened years ago, he became a liability. He probably told Cox about it. So Cox had to be killed and Montpellier too before he spilled any more beans.' He looked round triumphantly.

'This is a lot to get your head round on a Sunday morning,' Di Falco said. 'Could you explain cleared funds again?'

'I write you a cheque for a thousand pounds. You lodge it with your bank. It will not clear until my bank decides to honour it. That will take a few days. Looking at the cleared funds in your account, your bank won't give you the benefit of that thousand pounds until my cheque clears – if it does.'

'Right,' Di Falco said. 'Thank goodness everything's done electronically these days.'

'That's an interesting theory,' Flick said, 'but how do we prove it?'

Baggo shook his head. 'We don't have a hope. All the records will have gone and even if we had the paperwork it would take a skilled accountant months to build a case.'

Flick broke the silence that followed. 'So where does that leave us? We were under instructions to charge Cameron Smith with Cox's murder but I for one tend to believe him when he said he didn't strangle him ...'

Baggo cut in. 'And one of Waldron's defence team is sure he didn't kill Spencer.'

Flick said, 'We'll have to understand the relationships among the Jolly Boys and their wives and try to crack their united front.'

'Perhaps that journalist might be able to tell us something,' Lance suggested.

'Yes,' Flick said. Let's break for lunch and meet again at two. I need to think. By the way Alex, do we know who leaked the details about Cox's murder to the press?'

'No ma'am, and I doubt if we'll ever find out. I have put the word out that you're not best pleased.'

'I certainly am not, but we've more important things to worry about.'

As the others filed out, Lance and Baggo approached Flick. Baggo said, 'There's something you need to know about the journalist.'

13

'Tell me about the journalist later,' Flick had said, then headed for her office. She had to work her way through the implications of Baggo's theory and she wished her brain was not so fogged by tiredness. But she also needed food and phoned Di Falco, asking him to fetch sandwiches from one of the local supermarkets. As she ate, she studied newspaper reports of Waldron's trial on her computer.

In the cells Baggo and Lance confronted Osborne, whose furious expression gave way to delight when he saw Baggo.

'Baggo! What the hell are you doing here? Mate, you've got to get me out of here.'

Lance said, 'It's not as simple as that, Mr Osborne. You've been charged with assaulting a prominent local businessman on his own property and there's corroborated evidence against you. You'll have to appear from custody tomorrow. But I see no reason why you shouldn't get bail then.'

'Tomorrow? Prominent local businessman? That poncy git with spaghetti for hair, all piled up on top so he doesn't look like a slap-head? These lying bastards fitted me up. They call themselves Jolly Boys. Psycho

Boys, more like. It was self-defence. He'd hit me here.' He pointed to his jaw but any swelling didn't show up on the wobbly, highly-coloured flesh. 'And as for that loony who fired golf balls at me,' he pointed to the egg on the side of his head, barely visible through his greasy hair, 'he belongs in a secure unit somewhere.'

Lance said, 'The duty solicitor will be available to represent you. There is a solid crown case against you, on paper at least, whatever the truth of the matter.'

'Fuck that.' This was the first time Osborne had been on the receiving end of a trumped-up charge. It reinforced his new desire to become a crusader for justice.

'What paper are you representing?' Baggo asked.

'Why should I tell you? You're not helping me.'

'We can't help you right now. We can help tomorrow. With bail.'

Osborne wished he was back in Spain. His back ached, his piles troubled him, he needed a drink and a fag and would welcome a shower. 'I just said I was a journalist.' He spoke quietly. 'I've been hired by Mrs Smith, Waldron's daughter, to prove her old lag dad's innocence. And I'm supposed to do the same for her hubby, the bloke in the next cell. He says he's innocent too. I was going round the so-called Jolly Boys, rattling their cages, know what I mean?'

Baggo knew exactly what he meant, and he understood why McPhail should have felt like punching him.

Osborne continued, 'Why should I assault that

poncy git? I had no reason to. I hit a raw nerve, he reacted and I defended myself, that's what happened.'

Baggo thought for a moment then said to Lance, 'We need to have a word. Outside.' He nodded towards the cell door.

Lance shrugged then followed him out.

'Oi! What about me?' Osborne wailed as the door slammed.

Far enough away so they would not be overheard, Baggo spoke earnestly. 'He's on our side but Flick will refuse to have anything to do with him. He'll charge about like a bull in a china shop, creating havoc. I'd like to be able to control him. Flick plays by the book and she'll just re-interview the suspects, probably after the post mortems. I'm sure what happened in 1984 is crucial, but the trail is now very cold, they're smart and they have got their story straight. Plus they've eliminated their weak link. We need unconventional methods, a wrecking ball to unsettle them, and Flick wouldn't stand for that. Would you be prepared to leave Osborne with me and not tell Flick for a bit?'

'Hey, she's my boss. I don't want to go against her. She'll be mad when she finds out.'

'We tried to tell her and she didn't want to know. I'll take the blame. I'm not thinking of anything bad, just a bit of bluffing and trickery. Give me twenty-four hours with Osborne after he gets out tomorrow before we tell Flick. Then her re-interviewing might work. The alternative is getting nowhere using Flick's regular methods with Osborne chucking spanners into the works and making life difficult because we'll have no idea what he might do.'

'I don't like it.'

'I don't particularly like it, but we're trying to put right miscarriages of justice. Do you want to see the real murderer or murderers go free?'

Lance grimaced. 'All right, but I don't want to know what you plan to do.'

'That's why I'll go back to see him alone. Thanks mate. I'll see you at the briefing.' He patted his shoulder and headed for Osborne's cell.

'Where's laughing boy?' Osborne demanded when he saw Baggo was alone.

'We need to speak,' Baggo said as he sat beside Osborne on the hard shelf that served as a bed. 'You will want the Smiths to pay you?'

'Of course I bloody do. I wouldn't have come here otherwise.'

'With Cameron Smith in the next cell, they'll know you've been arrested, they'll lose confidence in you and refuse to pay. And no wonder. Have you made any progress?'

'A bit.' With a wriggle he transferred his weight from one buttock to the other.

'In other words, bugger all.'

Osborne shrugged.

'So this is what we do. I'm helping unofficially and that gives me some leeway. You help me, doing exactly as I say, and we have a chance of finding out who killed Spencer and framed Waldron. Then you should get paid as you'll have helped get the result the Smiths want. Agreed?' Baggo still found it difficult to speak assertively to his old boss but it was the only way to handle him.

Osborne tried to hide his relief; he had been close to despair. But he hated taking orders from someone he had once referred to as the tea-boy. 'All right,' he said with a show of reluctance, 'But I need to get the credit I deserve.' Baggo nodded. 'You don't have a fag on you, do you?'

'Sorry, I don't. I know you visited Montpellier yesterday. Tell me what happened.'

'He hit me on the head with a golf ball, that's what happened.'

'Did he tell you anything?'

'Not much. He's lost his marbles, I could see that. I asked if Waldron had killed Spencer and he just grinned. He said Waldron was too clever for his own good and Spencer, the victim, was slippery as an eel; he was a boozer and a serial shagger; he'd pissed off a few husbands. Oh, and he couldn't keep his trap shut. The Psycho Boys helped one another and McPhail, I take it he's the poncy git I'm supposed to have assaulted, couldn't have afforded to ditch his first wife if they hadn't helped out. I was going to keep going when his scary missus kicked me out.'

'And you went on to the McPhails?'

'Yes. Worse luck.'

'Did you learn anything?'

'Not much. They were talking about the bloke

who'd lost his marbles, saying what a liability he'd become. Stating the bloody obvious.'

'What did you make of them?'

'McPhail's no pushover. It's him who's made up the story to get me into the shit, you can be sure of that. His wife's younger, quite fanciable. She didn't say much. Harkins is a slap-head with ants in one armpit and no balls. His wife, Waldron's ex, acts cool as a cucumber so you wouldn't guess her shagging history. I might try to get her into bed, myself. Another notch on the bedpost.' He leered at Baggo.

'You're joking.'

'Only half, Baggo. You've got to smell the flowers along the way.'

'Have you seen Waldron?'

'He's bloody obsessed with proving his innocence. It makes no sense to me as he's going to pop his clogs any time soon. And he's no fool. Spencer's killing was well planned and he wouldn't have left the sodding murder weapon in his pocket for anyone to find. I bet he was verballed, too, but we won't prove that. He gave me piles of fucking papers, lawyers' arse-wipes, most of them. They're at the B and B they put me in. You can get them there if you want to. But why are you helping unofficially?'

'Because I too believe Waldron was wrongly convicted.' He wasn't going to tell his old boss about Melanie and her father.

Osborne shook his head. 'I'll never make you out, Baggo. Maybe one day you'll be a saint. If your elephant-gods have such things. Now tell me, what do you know?'

'For a start Montpellier was found dead, face down in a burn near his house this morning.'

'Fuck me. Was he bumped off?'

'We think so, but it's going to be hard to prove, particularly due to his mental state. The post mortem's tomorrow. The working theory is that the clue to Cox's murder and Montpellier's death goes back to the events of 1984. How we don't know.'

'We need to shake up the Psycho Boys. That's what we need to do. When I was cleaning up the East End and a gangster seemed bullet-proof, I'd bite his arse, make him squirm so he'd make a fucking mistake.'

This was exactly what Baggo knew he would say, and why Flick would have nothing to do with him. They swapped mobile numbers and Baggo promised to pick him up the next day once he had been bailed. He would explain his cheque cross-firing theory then.

* * *

'Let's proceed on the basis of Baggo's theory,' Flick said as the resumed briefing opened. 'Those involved in the cross-firing must have included McPhail. Montpellier knew about it and I assume he was involved too. Lightbody changed the subject when his wife started to talk about Czechoslovakia so probably knew about it, though Norma obviously didn't.'

'Cross-firing can work with more than two

participants,' Baggo said. 'Instead of a direct exchange it could be a money-go-round. A pays B, who pays C, who pays A. So long as they used different banks, of course. That would make it harder to spot.'

'Do we know what firms they worked for?' Flick asked.

'I looked that up over lunch,' Lance said, glancing at Baggo. 'McPhail managed East Neuk Properties Ltd. They specialised in low-end houses all over the Neuk. Montpellier was in his family firm, Montpellier and Montpellier WS. Very well regarded, lots of posh clients, trusts and so forth. Waldron was in another old St Andrews firm, Cradock Gill and Murdoch, known as Haddock Kill and Murder even before Waldron's conviction. His father had been a partner. The junior partner was Harkins.'

'Waldron was well respected before his arrest,' McKellar volunteered. 'The firm was on the up. It's barely ticking along now.'

Lance continued, 'Lightbody is in Reid and Fanshawe, a Crail firm, and he was there in 1984. Spencer was in L & P Campbell, a Cupar firm. They were taken over by Montpelliers soon after the murder and became a branch office. It's closed now.'

'Could we find out which banks they used?' Baggo asked.

Flick said, 'That shouldn't be difficult. Lance, you get on to that tomorrow. As I see it at the moment, the only person who we know benefitted from Waldron's conviction is Harkins, who stepped into his shoes in the firm and with his wife. Perhaps Spencer's death benefitted Montpellier by making it easier to take over his firm, but would a man like Montpellier murder for a branch office?'

No one answered.

Flick continued, 'Before we re-interview the suspects we need to have something to put to them. If we just ask them about cross-firing now they'll laugh in our faces. By tomorrow afternoon we should know where the different firms banked and Dr MacGregor will have done the post mortems. I'd like to have another briefing at twelve tomorrow. In the meantime, everyone should try and learn as much as possible about the Jolly Boys, gossip or not.'

As the rest filed out, Flick called McKellar back. 'Lance, please stay too,' she added.

'Sit down please,' she began hesitantly. She could see from McKellar's face that he knew what was coming. 'Mary Spencer said it was good to see you again.' She paused. 'She said your evidence was challenged by the defence at Waldron's trial. What was it that you told the court?'

'Is this official, ma'am, on the record?'

'I have to do it this way, Alex. You know that.'

Clearly feeling awkward, Lance shifted in his seat. McKellar pursed his lips. 'You'll do it this way anyhow. Well it's no secret, I was present when Detective Sergeant Thomson found the splintered golf tee in Waldron's jacket pocket. I also corroborated what the accused said in the car.'

'I'm sorry Alex, but I must warn you that anything you say may be taken down and used in evidence against you. You have the right to remain silent. Did Waldron say what you told the court he did?' She stared at him.

He fixed his eye on a spot on the wall past her shoulder and said nothing.

'Did Detective Sergeant Thomson really find the tee in Waldron's pocket?'

Now he looked her in the eye. 'He did. It was the fact it was wrapped in newspaper that drew attention to it.'

'Do you know if it had been planted there?'

'Not to my knowledge.'

Flick was relieved. 'You mean that?'

'Yes.' There was indignation in his voice.

'Right. Thank you both.' She needed to think.

After Lance had left, McKellar turned in the doorway. 'It was very different in those days. When you were a young officer you did as you were told. Or else. And the polis got results then. Bad guys were convicted. And if a youth did something wrong, he'd get a boot up the arse. It wasn't just about saving on paperwork. It taught most of them a lesson they didn't forget. And they didn't get a record. I can name a few upstanding citizens of these parts who can be grateful for old-fashioned policing.' Without waiting for a response he slammed the door behind him.

Flick held her head in her hands. If she started disciplinary proceedings it would open the way to a re-examination of Waldron's case; she was increasingly concerned that there had been a miscarriage of justice. But that could lead to a prosecution for perjury against McKellar; a man she had come to respect and trust would start his retirement in jail.

* * *

After leaving the briefing, Baggo drove to St Andrews where he visited the Lade Braes then The Scores, trying to get a feel for the places where two men had been found dead. Then he called at Osborne's B and B. The landlady regarded him with great suspicion. His explanation that her guest was visiting friends and would be back the next day caused her eyebrows to rise almost to her hairline. Clearly anxious about getting payment, she allowed him access to Osborne's room so he might pick up the papers only after collecting a hundred pounds from his credit card. The papers continued to give off a smell of jail. He had the driver's window open on the way back to Edinburgh – and Melanie.

14

'There's roast chicken for supper,' Fergus' mother told Flick as she sat down to spend some precious time with Verity. 'I've changed her,' Agnes Maxwell added as Flick sniffed the back of her daughter's nappy. 'There was nothing in the fridge,' she continued, her disapproval plain. 'I went to the supermarket and got plenty for the next few days.'

'How much was it?' Flick asked, trying not to sound sharp.

'Oh never mind. Our treat. You obviously need the money or you wouldn't be working on a Sunday.'

'I normally don't but there have been two suspicious deaths in as many days. So instead of doing my usual Sunday shop, I've been trying to find a killer. Where's Fergus?'

'I sent him off to the driving range since he hasn't had his golf this weekend. He'll have to work tomorrow, you know.'

She hadn't been in the house for five minutes and her mother-in-law had infuriated her already. She clamped her mouth shut, not trusting herself to remain civil.

'Are you making progress then?' Bernard Maxwell spoke for the first time.

'Some, but it's too early to make an arrest.'

'Well get a list of suspects and keep interviewing them. Sooner or later the guilty party will crack. It worked for me.'

Before he could ask about the details of the case, she scooped up Verity and carried her up to her bedroom where she read her a story, then another one, and another.

'Hello, darling.' Quarter of an hour later, Fergus came in and kissed her. 'Isn't mother doing a great job? Supper's nearly ready. Roast chicken!'

During the meal, Flick concentrated on spooning food into Verity, trying to ignore her in-laws.

'You won't consider buying a playpen, Felicity?' Agnes asked. 'Dad had to keep watch on her while I was busy in the kitchen. She's into everything.'

'Playpens make the child feel restricted,' Flick said.

His mouth full of chicken, Bernard said, 'She's fine in that high chair, but in the sitting room you need eyes in the back of your head. I don't understand these new-fangled ideas from London.'

'Not just London. Playpens just aren't used any more,' Flick snapped.

'I sometimes wonder why they're not used,' Fergus said, earning a glare from his wife.

As soon as Verity had settled, Flick went to bed. 'I've been up since six-thirty,' she said pointedly.

Fergus followed her up. 'Are you all right, darling?' he asked. 'You seem a bit crabbit.'

She took a deep breath, but this wasn't the time. 'It's been a long day and I'm tired. And I wish I could have spent the day with Verity,' she added, her voice catching.

'How's your inquiry going?'

She told him, step by step. He listened attentively. She concluded, 'So apart from suspecting these Jolly Boys I have no real leads. And I don't know what to do about Alex McKellar.'

'There's no need to rush into a decision on him. Wait and see what happens over the next few days. And assuming these two deaths are both murders, someone is badly rattled and desperate that the truth about what happened in 1984 should not come out. They'll probably make a mistake, or have made one already. That'll give you your opportunity.'

This was good advice but it didn't help her to sleep. She made a point of being the one to get up to tend to Verity when she cried.

The next morning, Fergus left the house first. Flick took Verity to nursery before going to work herself. The town was busy as South Street had been taken over by the Lammas Fair. A variety of rides and thrills were being quickly and skilfully set up, giving the historic old street a strange, vibrant, exciting atmosphere. On the way out of the nursery, she came face to face with Amy Smith, little Sandy holding her hand. Flick smiled politely but Amy Smith glared at her then turned her head away sharply. Oblivious to the unspoken exchange above him, Sandy asked, 'See Dadda later?'

As Flick left for work, she said a brusque goodbye to Fergus' parents. While Bernard grunted a response, Agnes took her arm. 'You mustn't mind us, dearie. We're a different generation and we did things differently. But we love our wee granddaughter; we'd do anything for her. And we love our son, and we know you make him happy. You're a good, devoted mother, we both see that. You just do it your way, as we used to. We don't want to intrude, but we're happy to help here for as long as you need us.'

Gulping back an unexpected tear, Flick said 'Thank you, Agnes,' and drove off before her emotions showed. By the time she reached Cupar she felt better but slightly guilty.

As soon as she had settled behind her desk, McKellar knocked at her door. He spoke stiffly, formally. 'I have a lady here I think you'll want to see, ma'am, Mrs Elizabeth McNaughton. She used to be Mr Montpellier's secretary.'

* * *

It was clouding over as Baggo drove north across the Forth Road Bridge offering a silent prayer to Ganesh, the elephant-headed god who brought good fortune to travellers. To his right, the iconic, red metal rail bridge, more than one hundred years old and still robust, defied the wear and tear of time. To his left, the stumps and towers of the new, twenty-first century bridge rose from the water. Rumoured to be on time and on budget, it would take the strain off the flawed suspension bridge, a mere half-century old, that carried all vehicular traffic between the Lothians and Fife.

Melanie had left early, their morning love-making quick and functional. Although a civil case was taking her to Kilmarnock, she was due to stay in the Ayr hotel used by the criminal bar, the proprietor's own bar profits more than recouping the discount he gave visiting advocates for accommodation. Baggo had distrusted most of the criminal advocates he had met and was uneasy about Melanie spending much time in their slick, sharp company. Despite her assurances that she would have to work every evening, he would be glad when she returned home. In the meantime he hoped that Lance Wallace might offer him a bed, saving him the daily drive to and from St Andrews. He had packed a bag just in case.

Waldron's papers had given him all the details about the trial that he had looked for. It was background that he wanted to know more about and he planned to visit Waldron before the twelve noon briefing.

His thoughts were interrupted by his mobile. It was a man called Hotchkis who explained that he was the duty solicitor in Cupar Sheriff Court. He was phoning about Noel Osborne. 'If he's to get bail, he needs a bail address. The address he gave me, a B and B in St Andrews, will not do. The landlady has refused to have him back as she doesn't want her house "dragged through the courts". Mr Osborne gave me your name. Would you be prepared to let him stay with you, even if just for a few days, till he can find somewhere else?'

Baggo's heart sank. 'If I say no?'

'Then he'll stay in custody till an address can be found.'

Baggo hesitated. There was no way that he wanted the appallingly slobbish Osborne as a house guest. But for the plan he had half formulated he needed him to be free. He thanked his lucky stars that Melanie would be away for two or three nights; she would not tolerate Osborne and would certainly throw him out of her flat. Perhaps Baggo too. His mouth dry, he gave Hotchkis the details he required. He was told he should be able to collect Osborne from the court about one o' clock.

He decided he would give Osborne the old sleeping bag he had used as a boy and let him sleep on the bed in the spare room, putting the used pillow-cases in the laundry basket. There would be no smoking; he would lock up alcoholic drinks. He would clean the bathroom thoroughly before Melanie got back. Most importantly, he would find somewhere else for Osborne to stay. With luck, Melanie would never know he had been there.

When Baggo reached St Andrews, the Lammas Fair was about to get underway and he had difficulty in finding a parking space. By the time he had walked to the Smiths' door in South Street, music was blaring and machinery was clanking. The first screams of terror from the thrill rides echoed off the old stone walls. He was unsure if the doorbell could be heard inside and so gave it an extra push.

The door opened a fraction and a tall woman with dark eyes set wide apart peered out. Behind her a dog growled.

'Mrs Smith? I'm Detective Sergeant Chandavarkar. I'd like to …'

'Do you have a warrant?' she demanded.

'No, but …' The door was slammed in his face.

He rang again but the door remained shut. Aware that passers-by were watching, he bent and shouted through the letterbox. 'I believe your father is innocent. Your husband too. I want to help.'

The dog began to bark but the door opened. 'Come in then,' the woman said.

The distrust on her face melted gradually as Baggo explained briefly why he needed to see her father. 'Well it can't do any more harm,' she said and showed him to a room at the back of the house. She knocked then opened the door. She did not go in with him. Inside, a tall man sat hunched in a wheelchair, doing nothing. He had the same dark eyes, set wide apart, as his daughter and the same snub nose. But whereas she was vibrant with a sunburnt complexion, he had a pallor that spoke of jail. And death. He looked at Baggo without curiosity, his eyes empty.

'Shut the door, please,' he said in a flat voice.

'Mr Waldron, I believe I can help you. I'm Detective

Sergeant Chandavarkar, but I'm pursuing my own line of inquiry.' He produced his warrant. Waldron barely glanced at it. Baggo continued, 'I think you were set up in 1984 and I need some background information from you about the Jolly Boys.'

'Don't bother.' The voice was clipped, more educated than Baggo expected from a man who had spent thirty years plus in jail.

'Don't bother? Why not?'

He looked up at Baggo. 'I've brought nothing but grief to my daughter since I came here. I don't want things to get worse for her.'

'Your release has brought matters to a head. I think I know some things about what happened years ago, but you have to help me. If I'm right, I hope I can prove that you were innocent and that your son-in-law didn't kill Cox.' Waldron remained impassive. Baggo continued, 'Look, I'm doing this in time I should be using to swot for my inspector's exam. I'm going out on a limb not just for you but for justice. Charles Arbuthnot has spoken to me about your case.'

Waldron looked surprised. 'Charles? A good man.' He frowned. 'We've already got someone who's supposed to be working for us but all he's done is get himself arrested.'

'But he's stirred things up and that may help us.'

Waldron shrugged. 'What do you want to know?'

'Tell me what Jocelyn Montpellier was like in 1984. I don't know if you've heard but he was found dead in a burn yesterday morning.'

Waldron showed no emotion beyond puzzlement. 'Joss dead? How did he die?'

'We don't know, but we suspect that he was murdered. He had dementia and had become very disinhibited, saying things about what happened in the past.'

'Anything about my conviction?'

'Nothing direct. But please, what was he like?'

Waldron frowned as he chose his words carefully. 'He was larger than life with a grand manner and a life-style to match. He was extravagant – fancy cars, expensive holidays in the South of France with his posh friends. He was definitely upper class but not really a snob; he treated everyone the same. He was bright and liked sparky, stimulating company. He was older than the rest of us and had come down from Oxford with a good degree. There was a group of us, all from Fife and doing Law at Edinburgh. We all played rugby and shared a flat in our last two years. Joss was our leader then and that sort of continued when we came back to Fife. We got up to all manner of things, pretty harmless most of them, though once we got our revenge on an opponent who had gouged Jimmy Lightbody's eyes in a scrum; we found out where he lived, ambushed him then stripped him and tied him to his club's flagpole with his underpants over his head.' He smiled. 'Then we all peed on him. It was a cold night too. It was a while before he was rescued. That was Joss' idea.'

Baggo smiled. 'What sort of a lawyer was he?'

'A good one, as you'd expect. He oozed confidence. He joined his family firm and they had lots of wealthy clients. He made sure he was on good terms socially with them and then charged exorbitant fees. He had a lot of low-value clients as well but I think he had the sense not to over-charge them.'

'Did your group help one other?'

'We did, referring clients to another Jolly Boy if there was a conflict of interest, that sort of thing. If one of us had a problem in their office we'd talk about it, offer advice.'

'I believe Kevin McPhail went into a property company. Did you know anything about your group helping him?'

Waldron thought for a moment. 'No.'

Baggo stared at him. 'Are you sure?'

Waldron's eyes flickered. 'I don't know what you mean.'

'At a restaurant on Friday night, Montpellier was pretending to shoot McPhail with McPhail shooting back. He said he'd got McPhail out of the shit and no one had lost. McPhail was annoyed.'

Waldron shook his head. 'Means nothing to me.'

'Do you remember the Whitchill Property case?'

Waldron nodded. 'Yes. It created a bit of a stir. Edinburgh solicitors were helping a property company by cross-firing cheques. Is that what was going on? I knew nothing about it. Honestly.' For the first time he looked directly at Baggo.

'I know it'll be almost impossible to prove, but yes, I believe that was what was happening.'

'Who do you think was involved?'

'McPhail, obviously, and almost certainly Montpellier. Maybe Lightbody as well. His wife told the police that Montpellier had mentioned Czechoslovakia in the restaurant and the officers noticed how quickly he changed the subject.'

'When Montpellier had actually talked about cheques? That would be right. Jimmy followed Joss like a puppy. Joss was easily flattered and liked to boss Jimmy around. Jimmy's wife, Norma, was never the sharpest tool in the box.'

'What about McPhail?'

Waldron grimaced. 'He was chippy. His father was a gardener and he had started with nothing. He married money, though.'

'Montpellier told someone he couldn't have afforded to get rid of his first wife without help from the Jolly Boys.'

'Indeed?' A hint of a smile passed over Waldron's face.

'His current wife is much younger. And pretty, I'm told.'

'There's a surprise.' Baggo saw he was relaxing. Waldron continued, 'Appearances were always important to him. That lunch on the last day of the Open was typical: no expense spared, Champagne, lobster, the lot. As well as us he had a couple of bankers and their wives. I remember thinking at the time it was a bit extravagant as there were rumours his company was struggling.'

'Do you think Spencer might have been involved

in the cross-firing? The more that were involved the more difficult it would be to spot.'

'Spencer was an untrustworthy bastard,' he replied forcefully. 'But no. He had a very loose tongue when he had a drink in him, which was frequently. No one in their right mind would involve him in a dodgy scheme.' He smiled. 'I remember once Joss called him "the Exorcist": if you invited him to your house, the spirits disappeared. He wasn't very pleased.'

'I know Spencer had an affair with your wife,' Baggo said softly, hoping not to stall the flow of information.

Waldron said nothing. Baggo waited. 'It was an infatuation. Susan thought it was serious but it wasn't. I knew.'

'How?'

'I just did.' He sniffed and wiped away a tear. 'I loved my wife, Mr Chan… Detective Sergeant. I'm a rational man and I've asked myself why many, many times and still have no answer. She was unfaithful, demanding, infuriating but I loved her and our little daughter. Totally, hopelessly. I would have put up with almost anything.' He paused. 'She'd done it before, fallen for someone and left me. But she came back and I forgave her. Deep inside, she knew I'd always be there and that we belonged together. Spencer might have taken her away, but she would have come back. I just know that. And I believe she knew that too.' Shaking with emotion, he asked, 'Have you ever been in love?'

Baggo nodded. 'Yes. I am, actually.' This was not the first time a complete stranger had unburdened themselves to him in a way they would not have done to friends. He felt obliged to reciprocate. He let Waldron collect himself. 'She married Hugh Harkins,' he said.

'She must have been desperate. A complete mismatch, but he's been good to Amy, so I suppose I should be thankful. He was always a plodder, my junior partner. He tagged along with us and hero-worshipped Joss, which was right up his street, of course.'

'Might he have been involved in cross-firing?'

'He would have had no scruples about it, but he knew I kept a close eye on the firm's accounts. So no, I don't think so.'

'That might have been a motive to frame you.'

Waldron shrugged. 'Putting it that way, I suppose so.'

'What about Spencer's wife, Mary I think? What was she like?'

'Plain, worthy. Far too good for Spencer. It was the peacock and the peahen. He was always well turned-out. He looked good and women found him charming. Didn't see it myself. She was dowdy, decent and homely. I believe she wanted children but he didn't. She put up with his nonsense but I don't know how she really felt. Now I'm getting tired.'

'Just one more question: Mrs Montpellier tried to keep her husband quiet when he was being indiscreet in the restaurant. Do you think she might have been involved in what was going on?'

'Definitely not. She was a restraining influence on Joss and would have put a stop to anything illegal and risky. Mind you, she knew how to spend money too but she wasn't reckless. Georgia's a strong woman and she could stand up to Joss. A weak woman would have bored him. The sparks could fly but they had a good marriage. If she knows more now, it will be because he's blurted it out recently because of his dementia.'

Baggo thanked him and was rewarded by a bony handshake with a surprisingly firm grip. On his way to the door another thought struck him. 'Sorry, one more thing, why did you collect these poisonous frogs?'

'I used to collect insects as a boy. The hobby sort of developed from there. I found these particular frogs fascinating, so tiny yet they carried enough poison to kill an elephant. You have to get wild ones as they get their toxicity from the ants they eat in the jungle. Those bred in captivity are not poisonous. I wanted the real thing. And much good it did me,' he added wistfully.

'And you say one was taken during the party you held a week before the Open?'

'It must have been then. And it could have been any of the people we've talked about.' He paused. 'Of course Susan could have taken one at any time. But I can't believe …'

'We can't make any assumptions.'

Waldron shrugged and turned away abruptly. 'Shut the door,' he commanded as Baggo left.

Baggo gave Amy a reassuring smile on his way out. 'I see it's raining,' he remarked.

'It always rains for the Lammas Fair,' she said gloomily.

15

Mrs Elizabeth McNaughton was a bird-like lady of about fifty, neat, precise and with an artificially refined accent. She sat on the edge of the chair facing Flick, her hands working nervously on a button-hole of her light wool cardigan.

Flick gave her an encouraging smile. 'I believe you have something to tell us about Mr Montpellier. We need to know as much as possible in view of the circumstances of his death.'

'I'm not comfortable about this, but Mr McKellar said it could be important.'

'Well?'

'I haven't told anyone about this. I worked in Montpelliers for thirty-five years and I was always discreet. You learn things in a lawyer's office that mustn't be talked about. Client confidentiality. That was the first thing I was taught when I started. More important than anything else.'

Flick forced herself to smile patiently. She could see that the woman was working herself up to break the habit of a lifetime.

'As Mr Montpellier's dead, I feel I can say this.'

'Yes?'

'Well, a bit before Mr Spencer was murdered, I'd noticed some strange things. There were files for clients we never met or even heard from. They were kept together at the back of the filing cabinet. These files related to property sales and there was just a couple of letters and a cheque, none of the usual things that arise, date of entry, whether the carpets are included and so on. There was even one for an address that didn't exist. I remember it, 3 Welford Way, Strathkinness. I knew there was no Welford Way and asked Mr Montpellier about it. He got cross, which wasn't like him at all, and told me it was going to be built soon. But it wasn't. I feel wrong telling you about this, because he was a wonderful man in many ways, always good to me.'

'Were these odd files connected with any particular company?'

She sniffed disapprovingly. 'East Neuk Properties. Mr McPhail.'

'Were you aware of money passing between Mr Montpellier and that company?'

'The letters I typed referred to cheques. I didn't write the cheques or anything.'

'Do you think these files might still be in existence?'

'No. Every couple of years we sifted through the cabinets and shredded dead files. Can you imagine the storage space we'd need if we kept everything?'

'Around the time we're talking about, was Mr Montpellier in touch more regularly than usual with any other solicitors in the area?'

'He'd always spoken a lot to Mr Lightbody. I did notice that Mr Spencer was trying to contact him quite often in the weeks before he was killed.'

'What about Mr Waldron?'

Her face clouded. 'They weren't in touch very often. Mr Montpellier was … well, wary of him. A few months before the murder he'd persuaded one of our best clients, Sir John Gladwell, to go to him. Mr Montpellier was furious.'

That was interesting. Casually, Flick asked, 'What about Mr Harkins? He was Mr Waldron's partner I believe.'

'I don't think they talked on the phone very often then. They did contact each other more after the murder. I wasn't the telephonist, you'll understand, but we chatted amongst ourselves. I never told anyone about these odd files before,' she added with emphasis.

'You obviously knew Mr Montpellier very well. Can you tell me what he was like?'

'He was a gentleman. And a character. He made me laugh. He could be irritating though. He worked in spurts. It was as if at times he couldn't be bothered and just upped and offed to play golf or whatever. At other times he'd work an eighteen-hour day. He was so clever and quick. He got through work much faster than any other lawyer I've known.'

'What did you make of Mr McPhail?'

'I thought he was rude. He didn't speak to us the way he spoke to Mr Montpellier. I heard Mr Montpellier call him Kid on the telephone. Mr Montpellier sort of patronised him.' She frowned and shook her head. 'I shouldn't be saying this, because Mr Montpellier acted for him in his divorce, but it was common knowledge: he was mean to his first wife. She had family money and he used that to build up his property business. Once the business started to do well, and it had gone through a rough patch, he left her and went off with someone much younger but not nearly as nice.'

Mrs McNaughton had effectively confirmed Baggo's cross-firing theory and given some useful background. Flick said, 'That's been most helpful. But what persuaded you to come forward as you've kept silent all these years?'

'Mr McKellar said what happened then might have some bearing on Mr Montpellier's death. And my son Luke and I owe him a lot. Luke was wild. One time it was under-age drinking and vandalism. Mr McKellar didn't charge him but he gave him a "talking-to". His ribs were sore for a couple of weeks. And he had to clean up what he'd done. That sorted him out. Now he's a casualty doctor in Dundee.'

Flick wished she hadn't asked. She picked up her phone and asked McKellar to show out his prize witness.

* * *

As she was mulling over what Elizabeth McNaughton had said, Flick's telephone rang. It was the pathologist.

'Good morning, Inspector. As I haven't heard from you today, I trust that the good citizens of St Andrews all slept safely in their beds last night?'

'I didn't. When you have a teething fourteen-month old, sleeping is something other people do.'

'Ah yes, I remember it well. But this time will pass. You'll probably want to know what I learned from the two gentlemen I have been examining this morning.'

'I can't wait.'

'Mr Cox first. Time of death was about two am, as we knew. There were four injuries that I found. There was an injury to the nose which cracked cartilage and caused bleeding. It would be consistent with a powerful punch, though almost any blunt force trauma might have caused it. The second injury was a blunt force injury to the back of the head. There were fractures to the bony structures there and some bleeding into the brain itself. The third injury was related to the second one and more serious. It was a contre-coup injury to the front of the brain. The brain sits within the skull and can be shaken about. Sometimes a severe blow to one part of the skull makes the brain move so that it collides forcibly with the opposite side of the skull. That had happened here, and the damage to the brain caused by the contre-coup injury would probably have been fatal without medical intervention. All this is consistent with Mr Cox being punched on the nose so that he fell back, possibly losing his footing on the kerb, and the back of his head striking the road with considerable force. The way the body was lying when I examined it would support this theory. But the bleeding into the brain which might have killed him was interrupted within a short time by the injury that did kill him. He was strangled by his own bow tie. From the angle of the bruising round the throat I deduce that the killer knelt by his head, tied a half-knot and pulled, probably with their hands close to the half-knot and pushing downwards using their body weight. The head injury would probably have caused unconsciousness but from the position of the hands when the body was found it seems that he tried to stop the strangling. That means that he must have at least partially regained consciousness.'

'So the killer might have been someone other than the person who punched him?'

'Indeed. I believe it all happened at about the same time but after the head injury there was enough time for blood to seep into the brain before his heart stopped. Perhaps five minutes but that is an educated guess, no more. My SOCO friends have told me there were no fibres from the assailant on Mr Cox's clothes. I would have expected there to be some if they had knelt on or straddled his chest. In addition I can tell you that, subject to comparison samples of bunker sand matching the sand found on him, my theory that he had been playing golf shortly before his death seems increasingly likely. Oh, and he had been drinking quite heavily. He was roughly five times the new drink drive limit.'

'Thank you Doctor. That's most helpful.'

'Unfortunately I cannot be so useful in respect of Mr Montpellier. Shortly put, he was drowned. Water from the burn was in his lungs. He had sustained an injury to his forehead, a laceration, almost certainly caused by striking his head on the sharp rock beside his body. There was no bony injury; that is the thickest part of the skull. Notoriously, Glaswegians use it for "kissing". It would have been enough to stun him so that he might have drowned without intervention, or, with little force, someone might have held his face under water. I could find no evidence of that happening but then I wouldn't necessarily expect to. He too had been drinking, but was only about three times the drink drive limit. The time of death is difficult to calculate because of the partial immersion of the body in water. The burn was not particularly cold, twelve degrees Centigrade, and as it was a mild night, the air temperature was about fifteen degrees for most of the time after death. It's difficult to tell how quickly the body would have cooled. Lividity, the staining of the lower areas of the body, was complete when I first examined him and rigor mortis was advanced but not complete. Death definitely took place before midnight. From examination of the stomach and small intestine, I believe he had eaten about two and a half to three hours before death.'

'I'm told he had his dinner between eight and half past.'

'Well that would make the time of death eleven o' clock approximately.'

'Well thank you Doctor, as always.'

'Not at all Inspector. Don't hesitate to ring me if you think I might help further. I wish you good hunting.'

* * *

The briefing had started by the time Baggo rushed into the room. Spider Gilsland was talking about frogs. 'Phyllobates terribilis, commonly known as the Golden Poison Dart Frog, comes from Colombia. Brightly coloured, often yellow, it is about two inches long and one frog has enough poison to kill ten people. The natives use it for hunting. The poison is contained in glands on the skin and if you expose the frog to heat it will exude a toxic fluid. The natives dip their arrows in the fluid and any creature hit by an arrow will die. The poison attacks the nervous system and leads to heart failure. That's what happened to Tony Spencer. The frogs are social animals and live in groups. From what I've managed to find out, Waldron kept about nine in a tank. They must have been obtained from the wild as those bred in captivity are not toxic. Apparently it's something to do with what they eat in the wild.'

'Did Waldron keep any other creatures?' Flick asked.

Spider replied, 'He did, snakes mostly, but the poisonous frogs were the stars of the show. You needed to wear gloves to handle them.'

Di Falco asked, 'Did he keep any horrible, creepy-crawly things like spiders?'

'Yes,' Spider replied then saw it was a windup. He threw a biro across the table at his friend. It missed and clattered harmlessly against the wall.

'Children!' Flick's eyes flashed.

'Sorry ma'am,' Di Falco said but once Flick had looked away he winked at Spider.

Baggo cleared his throat. 'So it would be quite simple for someone wearing gloves to reach into the tank the frogs were in and take one out. They would need only a small container to remove it. The Waldrons had a party at their house a week before the murder.'

Spider said, 'Yes. Someone other than Waldron could have taken a frog.'

Flick then narrated what Dr MacGregor had told her.

Baggo said, 'So if Montpellier died about eleven, the Jolly Boys effectively alibi one another?'

'Pretty well,' Flick said, 'but remember eleven's only an approximate time.'

'Still, it would be tight,' Baggo said.

'Yes, we have to face up to that,' Flick said. 'Moving on, I've been told that Cox's mobile and wallet have not been found yet. Lance, have you found out who banked with what banks?'

'McPhail's company banked with the Bank of Scotland, Montpelliers with the Royal. Cradock Gill and Murdoch, Waldron's firm, were with the Royal too. Reid and Fanshawe, Lightbody's firm, were with the TSB. Spencer's firm, Campbells, were with the Clydesdale.'

Flick said, 'So cross-firing involving all these firms would have been possible?'

Baggo said, 'Yes. The two firms banking with the Royal would have had to be careful but if it was a circular money-go-round they could have disguised it effectively. However I don't think that happened. I have just seen Waldron and he denied knowledge of cross-firing. I actually believe him. After all, if he'd known about it his defence would have been sure to raise it at his trial. Apart from anything else it would have muddied the waters and the defence love to do that. Of course, Harkins was in the same firm but Waldron says he kept a close eye on the accounts.'

'Does anyone have any gossip that might help?' Flick asked.

Di Falco said, 'My mother says the Jolly Boys weren't popular with quite a few people.' McKellar nodded agreement. 'They were arrogant' Di Falco continued. 'Mafia-like, she said, and she should know. I tried to get more out of her but she clammed up. I don't know why.'

'The press are behaving themselves so far,' Flick said. 'There's a big fuss over Cox but only a small item about Montpellier. No one seems to have linked the two yet. But what about that journalist who is supposed to have assaulted McPhail? He seems to have been looking into Waldron's conviction. These deaths must have made him suspicious. I wonder who he's working for. It's odd that no news organisation has been putting two and two together, or at least asking questions.'

As Lance opened his mouth to speak, Baggo cut in. 'I'll see him after he gets bail today and follow up anything that might help.'

'Well keep me informed,' Flick said. 'It looks more and more likely that Baggo's cross-firing theory is right but even with Mrs McNaughton there's simply not enough evidence. If we approach McPhail and challenge him, he'll laugh in our faces. We need a way in, a weakness we can exploit. Billy, you press your mother for details, names and so on. Impress on her how important it might be. Baggo, you do the same with the journalist. We'll meet for the next briefing at ten tomorrow. I don't want to start re-interviewing until we have something we can effectively use.' She paused. 'Cameron Smith will be appearing in court about now. His case will be continued for further examination and the fiscal will oppose bail. He'll appear again in a week's time. I think he probably didn't kill Cox and I believe we're the best people to investigate it and Montpellier's death. I don't plan to involve the central organisation unless I have to.' She was gratified to see heads nodding. The recent shake-up of the Scottish police force was not popular.

'I hope you know what you're doing,' Lance whispered to Baggo once they were out of the room. 'I have to work with her after this is all over.'

16

Osborne was waiting outside the court when Baggo arrived to pick him up. He seemed agitated. 'I need a crap. Badly. There's no way I was going to go in that shithouse.'

A tall gentleman in a dark pin-stripe suit was passing by. Baggo asked him where were the nearest public toilets. He gave the pair a quizzical look but directed them to a car park called Fluthers where there were toilets.

It was not far away. Osborne rushed into the Gents, leaving Baggo outside. The rain had gone off but the sky remained leaden and it was a dreich day. Hands in pockets, Baggo felt conspicuous hanging around as he rehearsed what he would say to his old boss. As the minutes ticked past, he hoped that Osborne would not need to visit his bathroom for the same purpose.

A man with a bulbous nose, a goatee beard and garlic breath started to chat him up. Monosyllabic responses did not put him off and Baggo was about to produce his warrant when his phone rang. It was Melanie.

'Melanie, my darling! How's your day been?'

'Very good, but what's with all the gushing?'

'I've missed you so badly since this morning.' The man with the goatee turned away and went into the Gents, presumably to try his luck there. Baggo sighed. 'I'll explain when I see you. I'm fine but how about you?'

'I'm very well. And I'll be home this evening. We've just hammered out a settlement. I'm due in court soon to tell the sheriff but I thought I'd ring you. You'll be back, won't you?'

'Em, yes.'

'Great. Chinese carry-out with some Chablis? Oh, the case is calling. See you later.' She rang off, leaving Baggo with a sinking feeling in his stomach.

'Better out than in. I'm fighting fit now.' Osborne clapped him on the back. 'But I need fags.' On their way to Baggo's car, Osborne went into a general store and emerged with two packets of cigarettes, a pack of sandwiches and a half bottle of whisky. Standing on the pavement, he took a generous slug then lit up.

'Hey, no more booze. We have work to do.' Baggo tried to grab the bottle but Osborne was too quick for him.

'All right, all right. I know what I'm doing.' He took another swallow then reluctantly screwed the top on and put it in his jacket pocket.

Once they were in the car, between mouthfuls of sandwich, Osborne said, 'That Mrs Smith phoned me when I was in the bog. She wants progress. How can I make fucking progress when I'm banged up on a trumped-up charge? I told her I was working on something important and I'd phone her tomorrow.

I hope you've got something I can give her. She's a tough cookie.'

'I think I have.' Baggo explained his cross-firing theory, making sure Osborne understood.

They stopped in St Andrews for Osborne to pick up his suitcase from his former landlady. Baggo told him to ask for change from the hundred pounds he had had to pay to collect the papers. 'And see if she'll take you back,' he added more in hope than expectation.

A few minutes later Osborne returned. 'That was a waste of oxygen. The tight-arsed old dragon made me as welcome as a fart in a lift. And there was no way she was going to give me any money.' Baggo didn't know whether to believe him.

Taking a circuitous route to avoid the Lammas Market, Baggo took a road out of town to the south. 'Where are we going?' Osborne asked.

'Crail. It's a picturesque little place down the coast. And you're going to visit a lawyer there.'

'Some hot-shot sleaseball who'll get me off my assault charge?'

'No, a man called Lightbody. He's a partner in Reid and Fanshawe. I believe he was involved in the cross-firing.'

'What do you want me to say to him?'

Baggo told him. By the time he had finished they were driving along old, narrow streets. But in the steady drizzle, Crail looked drab rather than picturesque. As Baggo tried to find a parking place, Osborne asked, 'Do I use my own name?'

'Better not. He might identify you as the journalist before you're able to talk to him. Why don't you call yourself … Cameron?'

'David Cameron?'

'Too common. What about … Jeremy?'

'Me a Jeremy? You having a laugh?'

'Suit yourself then.'

'You'll wait here?'

'Of course. Good luck.'

Osborne got out of the car and immediately headed for a shop doorway where he lit up. After a few deep drags he walked round the corner to Lightbody's office. Baggo brought out his phone and googled bed and breakfasts in St Andrews.

* * *

Reid and Fanshawe's receptionist was a cheery lass who looked as if she seldom strayed far from a cream bun. Osborne, who found wobbly female flesh attractive, wiped the welcoming smile from her face with a toothy leer.

'Can I help you?' she asked coldly.

'I'm here to see Mr Lightbody.'

'Do you have an appointment?'

'No, but he'll want to see me.'

'Your name?'

'Cameron, Fred Cameron. I've some important information about the late Mr Montpellier.'

'He's with a client at the moment.'

'I'll wait.' He took a seat on one of the three wooden chairs against the wall to the receptionist's right. It afforded a good view of all the doors leading off the foyer. He folded his arms and settled down to wait, his eyes drawn to any movement at the front of her too-tight shirt as she typed on a computer or answered the phone.

Twenty minutes passed then a door opened and a lady with a capacious handbag thanked Lightbody by name and left. Before the dapper little man with the wrinkled face could retreat back into his room Osborne was beside him. 'I have to speak to you, Mr Lightbody. It's urgent and concerns the late Mr Montpellier.'

Covered in confusion by this forceful approach, Lightbody stammered, 'All right, but I'm very busy this afternoon.'

Osborne followed him into his room and shut the door. The first thing that struck him was the number of filing cabinets. Half a dozen of them stood against one wall, two against another. The rest of the furniture was old-fashioned brown wood, all polished. Behind the large desk was a leather swivel chair which, turned to the left, would give a fine view out to sea. On the desk, and precisely arranged, was a blotter, a black, lacquered tray containing pens and pencils and a silver-framed photograph of a group of about ten men and women, strategically turned so it could be seen from both sides of the desk. There was a laptop and a phone on one side of the blotter, wire In and Out baskets on the other, both containing a few sheets of paper, letters mostly. In the middle, beside the tray for pens, was a curling trophy; two small granite stones sat on either side of an upright pen-holder. To Osborne's eye it seemed absurdly phallic but he doubted if that had occurred to the serious-looking Lightbody.

Osborne took the still-warm chair facing the desk recently vacated by the lady with the handbag. Knowing the intimidating potential of silence, he watched as Lightbody fussily tidied the file on the blotter and carefully slotted it into place in one of the filing cabinets then perched on the edge of the swivel chair and smiled nervously. 'How can I help you, Mr…?'

'You can call me Fred Cameron.' He paused, enjoying the sense of the other man's growing apprehension. 'I know.'

A facial twitch. 'Know what?'

'About the cross-firing.'

'What cross-firing?' An unconvincing expression of amazement.

Osborne smiled. 'Back in 1984. You've still got your marbles, unlike your late friend. You do know exactly what I'm talking about.'

'I don't. Please leave now, whoever you are.'

'If I do, you'll be named. And shamed.'

'You wouldn't dare.'

Osborne smiled. He was enjoying himself. This was like having a villain from the East End on toast.

'Have you heard of the internet? You can find it on that box.' He nodded at the computer.

Lightbody said nothing.

'East Neuk Properties, Montpelliers, Reid and Fanshawe, a merry money-go-round, conning the bankers that East Neuk Properties were doing a roaring trade, with lots of cash, while all the time they were skint and should have been put out of business.'

'That could never be proved … because it didn't happen,' he added.

'How do you think I got to know this? Because I have a witness. I've got them on video. I can have that in cyber-space any time. Actor's voice, silhouette, the usual. I'd send the link to the Law Society, the police, your best clients, anyone who fucking matters.'

Lightbody put his head in his hands and breathed deeply. 'Why are you here? What do you want?'

'I take that as an admission.'

'Well, what do you want?' Lightbody had meant to sound impatient but his voice quavered.

'Peter Waldron did not kill Tony Spencer. We both know that. But who did?'

'I don't know. Honestly. It wasn't me. It wasn't.'

'The murder had something to do with the cross-firing, which Waldron didn't know about.'

'I tell you, I don't know.'

Osborne stared at him and wondered if he might be telling the truth. 'Here's what will happen. If you don't tell me who the real killer was, my new website,

Criminal Lawyers, will expose the cross-firing tomorrow, Tuesday. It'll be the launch of the website and I want it to start with a bloody great splash. You, Kevin McPhail and the late Mr Montpellier will be named. On Wednesday I will give my views about which one of you killed Spencer. It's always been the rule that you can't libel the dead, but now, with the internet, I can speak the truth about anyone without exposing my arse. You, on the other hand, will be totally fucked. You know that. All the red-top papers will pick it up. They'll be able to name Montpellier and it'll be easy to guess who the others are.'

Lightbody swung his chair round towards the sea. Grey and menacing, it gave him no comfort.

'If I tell you who the killer was, will you leave me out?'

'How did you guess? That's the deal.'

'How can I trust you?'

'You can't. But remember two things. One, revealing the true killer after all this time, with a man wrongly imprisoned, makes the cross-firing fucking irrelevant, except as background. Two, journalists have always protected their sources and although I work on the internet, I'm still a bloody journalist and I have my principles.' Osborne, well into the part he was playing, puffed out his chest.

'I need time.'

'I can't give you much. Ten tomorrow morning.'

'How do I get in touch?'

'Phone me.' He rattled off his mobile number,

which Lightbody noted on a pad he removed from a drawer.

'And don't fuck me about. If you do, I'll make you pay.' He got up then remembered something Baggo had said. 'And I need more than a name. I need details, chapter and bloody verse.' With a final, threatening look at the stricken Lightbody he left, the door swinging behind him. He winked at the receptionist on the way out.

* * *

'He'll blame Montpellier,' Osborne told Baggo as they drove out of Crail. 'Poor bugger, just because he's dead and can't be libelled. He was pitiful, you know. When his missus called him in to eat he said he thought he'd had his supper. No wonder he looked like a bloody scarecrow, if he forgot to feed himself.'

'But Lightbody was rattled?'

'A brown trouser job. He pretty well admitted the cross-firing.'

'Then it's not so much whom he names but what he does. Hopefully in his panic he'll contact the others and we can stand back and watch the fur fly. Well done, by the way.' He smiled at his old boss.

Unused to compliments, at first Osborne didn't know what to say. He shrugged. 'It was good fun. Reminded me of the old days.'

'And he has till …?'

'Ten tomorrow morning.'

'And he has your number?'

'He noted it down as if his bloody life depended on it.'

'We'd better not leave St Andrews tonight.' This was the better of bad options; a night with Osborne in St Andrews was preferable to a thermo-nuclear explosion from Melanie if she had him foisted on her as a house guest. The only trouble was that all the bed and breakfasts were full. He pulled into a farm road and resumed googling. Five minutes later he was on the phone to a newly-opened Premier Inn on the Largo Road in St Andrews. Their single and twin rooms were taken but they had a double room available for a reasonable price. Baggo had slept on a few floors in his time and there was no way he would share even an Emperor-size double bed with Osborne. He took the room. Unhappy yet relieved, he phoned Melanie. Presumably on her way home, she did not answer so he left a message: the Chinese carry-out and Chablis would have to wait.

17

'It didn't do to cross them,' Heather Fabroni told Flick. A woman of about sixty who had not troubled to disguise the passage of time, her sagging bosom was compensated by a natural complexion neither weathered nor particularly wrinkled. Di Falco had gone straight from the briefing to his mother. She had reluctantly referred him to Heather, a Scottish girl who had married into the local Italian immigrant community and who had worked in the cash room of L & P Campbell, Tony Spencer's firm in Cupar. It had taken some persuading but now, with Di Falco at her side, she was in Flick's office talking about the Jolly Boys.

'This might be very important, so please tell us what you remember,' Flick said.

'I can't give you many details, but in the office we talked about some of the tricks they got up to.'

'Yes?'

'They practically drove a couple of young lads who were setting up in competition out of town. Conlon and Clarke, they were called. Mr Montpellier had something on one of the sheriff clerks. Bobby, our office boy, once heard Mr Spencer say to this clerk,

"If you don't do it, I'll tell Mr Montpellier." The sheriff clerks have a lot of power. They decide when cases call and give, or don't give, advice to solicitors about what's needed. And they have access to the sheriff. They can poison his mind about a particular lawyer. That's what happened with Conlon and Clarke. They were getting nowhere in Cupar and moved to Dundee, where they're doing very well.'

'So Mr Spencer and Mr Montpellier were responsible for squeezing them out?'

'That's what we all thought.'

'Anything else?'

'There was a member of the Licensing Board who was always coming to the office. Our firm, Campbells, and Montpelliers and Reid and Fanshawe were recognised as the specialists in licensing. Their clients always seemed to be successful, whether they were applying or opposing. I always felt there was more to it than expertise.'

'You suspect bribery?'

She shook her head. 'I can't say because I don't know. But I'm sure there was something.'

'What about Mr Waldron of Cradock Gill and Murdoch? Did Mr Spencer have many dealings with him?'

'He was supposed to be a friend of Mr Spencer's but Mr Spencer didn't like him after a couple of clients took their business to him.'

'And after Mr Spencer was murdered, Montpelliers took over the business?'

'Yes, as a branch office. And there was no need to shut it down. If they'd put in a young assistant full time, we'd have done fine. When I say they, I mean Mr Montpellier. He ran things.'

'Did you lose your jobs?'

'Yes. It came at a good time for my family, the children were young, but it was very bad for some of my work-mates. And they were terrible over redundancy. They made it as difficult as possible for us to get what we were entitled to.'

'Why were you so reluctant to tell us this?'

'Long ago, my husband's family suffered after one of them informed on the Mafia. He believes in letting sleeping dogs lie. Some of the people involved are still alive.'

Flick saw that speaking out had taken real courage. 'I understand. Thank you very much. Billy will give you a lift home.'

She took his arm and squeezed. 'No offence to Billy, but I'd rather take the bus.' There was a troubled expression on her face as she left.

* * *

'So who did kill Spencer?' Osborne asked as, munching a fried onion ring, he cut into a sirloin steak in the Premier Inn restaurant.

Baggo looked across the table at him. 'You tell me.'

His old boss had been acting out of character, taking a shower, shaving, having a couple of hours' sleep, putting on a change of clothes. Now, over dinner, he was happy to split a bottle of red wine; 'Let's not over-do it, we may have to work tonight,' he had lectured Baggo, then demanded to be brought up to date with the inquiry. The clapped-out old dinosaur had rediscovered his mojo.

Absent-mindedly scratching his crotch under his napkin, he said, 'As you know, I get gut feelings. I've met these so-called Jolly Boys and the only one with balls is that poncy property man, McPhail. I was bloody rude to the twitchy slap-head, Harkins, the one who married Waldron's wife. He jumped to his feet but he was never going to take a swing at me. As for prune-face Lightbody, he just folded this afternoon. I've known a lot of murderers, Baggo, and it takes guts to make a pre-meditated kill.' He paused to take another mouthful of blood-red steak.

'They might have been braver thirty years ago.'

'Na. Your basic nature doesn't change. It's just better hidden.'

'So you reckon it was McPhail who murdered Spencer? Or was it Montpellier?'

'Right. One or other of them. Of course Montpellier had changed. He used to be the main man, so he probably had the balls to do it back then. But he wasn't the man he used to be. He'd become a liability. Assuming he was bumped off, it must have been to stop him spilling any more beans. And Cox, let's take it Montpellier had told him who really had killed Spencer, he needed to be silenced quickly. So yes, I'm looking at McPhail for all three murders.'

Baggo said, 'So you reckon McPhail must have followed Cox from Harkins' flat? He had his car and would have had to drive up North Street. There is a lane that runs from North Street to The Scores. He could have used that lane and waited for Cox to walk along.'

'That's probably what happened, and he had a stroke of luck because Smith became involved and knocked Cox out. All the killer had to do was strangle him. But Baggo, the important thing is, whoever the killer was, he had followed Cox from the Harkins' flat prepared to do the whole job. In other words, he needed balls, so McPhail.'

Baggo said, 'So McPhail killed Spencer and then Cox, but remember, all the Jolly Boys alibi each other for the time Montpellier died, or at least the timing would have been very tight.'

Osborne chewed thoughtfully. 'I'll have to think about that.'

'We haven't mentioned the women.'

'The tarty Mrs Harkins, kill her lover? What are these plants that eat insects?'

'Venus Fly-Trap.'

'I don't see it. She's a shagger, not a killer.'

'Mrs Montpellier? Waldron told me she's a strong character but wouldn't stand for dodgy, risky dealings, so I can't see her killing Spencer. And Flick said she was distraught when her husband was found dead.'

Osborne nodded. 'McPhail had a different wife

when Spencer was killed. Of course the second wife might have helped him with the other two murders.'

'That would be unlikely, I think. No one seems to rate Lightbody's wife and she appeared not to know about the cross-firing; she talked about Czechoslovakia being mentioned in the restaurant, which was a big give-away.'

'I wonder what they're all doing now,' Osborne said. 'Running about like headless chickens, shitting themselves most like.'

At that moment, his phone beeped. He showed Baggo the text that had come in: 'South Street behind Terminator 10.00 pm'.

Baggo grimaced. 'He's smart. With all the noise of the fair, there's no way you'll be able to record what he says on your phone.'

18

The rain had eased by the time Baggo and Osborne left the hotel to walk uphill to South Street. Osborne, wearing a lurid orange, showerproof jacket, was highly visible. Baggo had a dark, quilted jacket, ideal for blending in with the crowd. When they reached the West Port, the ancient gateway to the town, Baggo told his old boss to go ahead. 'I won't be far away and I'll keep an eye on you,' he promised.

'I've been to fucking funfairs before,' came the reply as Osborne strode through the grey, stone archway into South Street.

But this was a funfair like no other. The lights and blaring music from the rides bounced off the old buildings. The road and the pavements shone black and wet from the rain. The crowd, enthusiasm undampened, laughed and shrieked with terror as a variety of exotic contraptions propelled them up, down and round about.

They had time to spare before ten. Osborne slowly made his way along the street, looking for the Terminator. Some of the rides were genuinely scary; one machine thrust people in a pod at the end of a metal arm skywards above the roofs of the buildings.

A girl emerging from the pod held on to the boy beside her for support. He smiled weakly, pretending to be unshaken.

More than half way along the street, not far from the Smiths' house, Osborne found the Terminator. He watched, fascinated, as about a dozen people sat in a row, secured by a bar in front of them. The machine then swung them back and forward, up and down, the row of seats rotating. When it stopped and the restraining bar was lifted, they staggered off, pale-faced but pretending to be unaffected. 'You coming, mate?' the operator shouted at Osborne as the next load of victims queued to take their seats.

'Not bloody likely,' Osborne replied and wandered away. He checked his watch; it was only quarter to ten. The rain came on again. He wished he had a hat. He spotted a van selling candy-floss. That was more like it. He bought a stick and, standing back from the Terminator queue, enjoyed the long-forgotten, sickly-sweet taste as he watched for Lightbody.

He had nearly finished his candy-floss when he felt a hard punch on the left side of his back. Then his chest was sore … he felt woozy … the Terminator seemed to be about to swallow him up … the wet pavement came up and hit him in the face.

* * *

Baggo had followed Osborne along the street. He had reached the Terminator well before ten and didn't want to be spotted as an observer. Next to the Terminator was an octopus-like roundabout, the Twister, with pods at the end of its tentacles. He paid for a ride and, as he was thrown about, was able to catch glimpses of Osborne's orange rain jacket.

When he got off, slightly giddy, he saw a group of people gathering where Osborne had been. He looked in vain for the orange jacket. Sensing that something was wrong, he rushed to see what had happened and pushed his way through the press of bodies.

Osborne lay on his front. He wasn't moving. The slim, brown handle of a knife stuck out of his back. A small pool of blood and candy-floss gathered beside his open mouth. 'I'm a police officer. Has anyone phoned 999?' Baggo shouted.

A woman's voice said 'I have'. A man bent and reached for the knife.

'Leave it,' Baggo yelled. 'If you take it out he'll bleed to death.' Pushing the man aside, he knelt beside Osborne. 'Noel, Noel, can you hear me?'

Osborne opened his eyes and groaned.

Baggo tore off his jacket and placed it over Osborne's back, carefully avoiding the knife. 'Stay with us, Noel, stay with us.'

Osborne groaned again. 'What …?'

'You've been stabbed, mate. An ambulance is on its way.' Baggo got his phone and called 999. 'Yes, I've been told someone's called already. I'm a police officer. It's very, very urgent … A man's been stabbed in the back … Yes, he's still breathing … St Andrews,

South Street, near its junction with …' 'Church Street,' a woman said. 'Church Street,' he added.

The call over, he forced himself to calm down, to think. He knew this was his fault; there would be hell to pay, particularly if Osborne died. If the handle was anything to go by, it was a steak knife, quite long and sharp. It must have gone near the heart. He looked up at the people gathered round. 'Please no one move,' he shouted. 'We'll need to question all of you.' Then he phoned Flick. 'There's been a stabbing at the Lammas Fair,' he told her. 'Junction of South Street and Church Street. It's connected to our inquiry. The victim's badly injured and an ambulance is on its way.' He couldn't bring himself to tell her who the victim was.

* * *

Flick was in bed and nearly asleep when the call came. She got up and dressed quickly, questions running through her brain. Who had been injured? How had Baggo managed to be there when it happened? How did he know it was connected to the inquiry? What had he been doing behind her back? She phoned Lance Wallace at home, telling him to organise SOCOs and a photographer. He said he would meet her at the scene. As it was raining, she put on a waterproof with a hood. Fergus gave her a lift, circling the streets blocked by the fair and dropping her off at the far end of South Street. 'Just as well Mum and

Dad are here for Verity,' he reminded her. 'Good luck,' he added. She kissed him then walked briskly past the attractions until she came to the knot of people beside the Terminator. While Baggo was talking to a man in the crowd, a blonde woman knelt beside the man on the ground. Flick recognised her as Jude Innes, the proprietor of the book shop in front of which the drama was taking place.

'His name's Noel,' Jude told her. Flick looked at the man's face, half-turned to his side. She didn't believe her eyes. It was her old nemesis, Noel Osborne, Inspector No, who had made life hell for her in Wimbledon CID. She glared at Baggo, who looked away sharply.

She would deal with him later. She had to be professional. She questioned a slightly drunk middle-aged man who was sure he had seen a tall youth in a hooded jacket running from the scene, along South Street towards the West Port. He had glimpsed his face and thought he might recognise him. After taking his contact details, she spoke to a girl who looked as if she was still at school but had been drinking. She was adamant that a bald-headed man had been beside the man in the orange jacket before he fell. The boy with his arm round her waist agreed with her. They didn't know if they would recognise the bald man. Neither of them had been aware of any tall youth nearby at the time of the stabbing. This was the usual problem with eye-witnesses to a situation involving sudden violence; it was almost impossible to guess which ones had accurately observed the event and which ones, with the best will in the world, had simply got it wrong. Flick was taking the details of the girl and boy when, with siren blaring and lights flashing, the ambulance came round the corner from Church Street.

Flick stood back, impressed as she always was by the calm professionalism of the paramedics. Talking reassuringly to Osborne, they lifted him into the ambulance, taking care not to do anything that might cause the blade to move about in his chest. 'We'll take him back to Ninewells,' the driver told Flick. With more noise and flashing lights, a police car driven by PC Austin arrived from Cupar. Flick told him to drive ahead of the ambulance to clear the road to Dundee.

As the ambulance left, Lance Wallace arrived in a second police car. At Flick's direction, he taped off the area where Osborne had lain and, with Baggo, they continued to interview members of the public. A photographer and Scenes of Crime Officers arrived. After speaking to them, Flick turned to Baggo. 'We'll sit in the police car. You come too,' she said, looking at Lance.

She sat in the driver's seat, Baggo took the front passenger seat and Lance, dreading what was coming, sat in the back.

'Well?' she said, pent-up fury in her voice.

Baggo made a silent prayer to Ganesh then said, 'This is down to me. Osborne was the journalist who is supposed to have assaulted McPhail. He had been engaged as a private investigator by Amy Smith to try and clear her father before he dies and now her husband too. If we'd left him to his own devices he'd have charged about like a bull in a china shop, getting in the way of what we were doing. This afternoon after he had got bail, I took him to Lightbody's office in Crail and he put the frighteners on him, saying that he had a website that would reveal the cross-firing, naming names, and saying who he believed had murdered Spencer in 1984. He told Lightbody that, as it would be on the internet, he would have been safe but the allegations would stick. He gave him till ten tomorrow morning to tell him who had killed Spencer. This evening he got a text, telling him to meet at the Terminator at ten tonight. We both expected Lightbody to come and thought he had selected the fair as a meeting place so that, with the background noise, we would not be able to record what he said. But we were wrong. I'm really sorry.'

'And you didn't tell me because?'

'I knew you wouldn't sanction it.'

'I or we?' She turned to Lance. 'Did you know about this?'

'Sorry, ma'am. Yes, I did.'

'I persuaded him,' Baggo added quickly.

Through gritted teeth, 'You promised me there would be no maverick stunts. And you, I … I trusted you.'

'Sorry,' they both muttered.

'Sorry doesn't cut it, doesn't begin to cut it. You've

done this before, making fun of me because I do things properly, as they're meant to be done. But this time it's gone wrong for you, and someone will have to be blamed. That someone will be me; I won't have been in charge of my inquiry; I'll have allowed unaccountable people to do their own thing with disastrous results. And you know what, you'd never have dared do this if I'd been a man. I'm trying to be a mother, a wife and a detective inspector, and I can't remember when I had a decent night's sleep. And two men, yes, men I liked and trusted have thought "she's only a woman, we don't need to respect her, certainly not obey her". And of course I'm English.' She glared at Lance. 'Well, you can both go to hell. You,' she turned to Baggo, 'don't do another thing in this investigation. And I hope you fail your inspector's exam.' Her voice caught. She was thankful that the dim light in the car would not reveal the tears that began to roll down her cheeks. But she felt better for her outburst.

What she said about disrespecting her because she was a woman went far beyond what Baggo had expected. It was nonsense, and she knew it. He opened the door and, as he got out, said stiffly, 'I'll e-mail you my report tomorrow.'

After the door slammed there was a moment's silence. Lance said, 'That was over the top, ma'am. We both really respect you and I think you know that. As far as I'm concerned you're probably the best boss I've had. You're intelligent, fair and sympathetic. You're a modern police officer but you don't just push a pen, you get the job done. And Baggo is bright, inventive and good at catching criminals. When you work together you're a truly great team. You know that too. In this case we all agree there has probably been a terrible miscarriage of justice, with a man who is dying desperate to clear his name and the real murderer still at large and continuing to kill to protect himself. What happened to Osborne shows that Baggo's plan has struck a nerve. If ever there was a time for working together it's now. Sorry for being so direct, ma'am.'

Flick made herself calm down. Something inside her told her Lance was right. But she was reluctant to back down. 'Too late,' she said.

'It's never too late to do the right thing, Flick, ma'am,' he said softly.

She thought for a moment then got out her phone and called Baggo's number. There was no reply. She didn't leave a message.

19

Baggo was fuming as he walked along Church Street away from the car. He had never played the race card against Flick and she had no business playing the feminist card against him. As he reached South Street, the operator of the Terminator was shouting that the last ride of the night was about to start. There was a space free. Baggo paid his money and took it. The experience was exhilaratingly terrifying and he felt better for it. When he got off, he checked his phone. There was one missed call, from Flick. He put the phone in his pocket and began to walk back to the hotel. He had not gone far before he had second thoughts and called her back.

'Hello,' she said. 'We need to work together.'

He said nothing.

'I shouldn't have said some of the things I said.'

'No.'

'But I'm still mad at you.'

'Understood.'

'But we have to work together. Now.'

Silence then, 'I'll be back at the car in five minutes.'

He walked slowly and climbed in. Facing straight ahead, he said, 'I told you already this was my fault and I accept blame for what has happened. Osborne was, is, a plonker but he was injured trying to put right something that went wrong a long time ago. He had the guts to challenge these people, who clearly have something to hide. And he's paid for it. I hope you'll give him credit for that.'

Full of conflicting emotions, Flick forced herself to think clearly. Eventually she said, 'What's done has been done. We have to get on with things. As you've got us into this mess, how do you suggest we get out of it?'

'I don't know if you noticed the handle of the knife? It was bone, dyed brown, quite slim and pointed at the end. Distinctive. I bet it's part of a set. If one of the Jolly Boys has an odd number of similar steak knives, we'll be getting somewhere. Whoever did this made a big mistake not pulling the knife out and taking it with him – assuming it was a man.'

'Good point. Did any of the people you spoke to see anything relevant?'

Baggo said, 'No. A few saw Osborne falling. Most thought he was having a heart attack.'

Lance said, 'There was a woman who saw a youth running down South Street. She was vague about his height, what he was wearing, everything.'

Flick said, 'A man I spoke to saw a tall youth wearing a hooded jacket running, also down South Street. A young couple had a bald man beside Osborne before he fell. Harkins is bald.'

Lance asked, 'Do you think the ambulance will have reached the hospital yet?'

Flick said, 'Let's find out.' She phoned Austin, who answered. 'So he's still alive? Good. Stay there till he's been treated and keep me posted. Now, when they remove the knife I want you to seize it, preserving evidence as well as you can. There probably won't be fingerprints, but you never know. I also want you to use your phone to photograph the knife, alongside a ruler, and send it to me. Please also speak to the surgeon who operates on him and ask what degree of force would have been required. Remember the blade had to pass through a waterproof jacket and whatever he had underneath. Also, try to find out whether or not they expect him to pull through. If he survives the operation, they'll say his condition is critical, but try to find out what they really think.'

Baggo interjected, 'Tell him to bring Osborne's phone back.'

She nodded, repeated what he had said, then ended the call and turned to the others. 'What now?'

Baggo said, 'I'd like to search all the Jolly Boys' houses tonight before they have time to get rid of knives that match the one used on Osborne, dry wet clothes, or even destroy any papers that relate to the cross-firing. There wasn't much blood coming from the wound, but there might be traces on the attacker's cuff.'

Flick said, 'We'd need warrants.'

'Hopeless Humphrey would never grant warrants for such wide searches; he'd call it "fishing"', Lance said gloomily. Sheriff Humphrey Logan, the local judge for that part of Fife, had earned his nickname from the police because of his dogged insistence in seeing good in the worst recidivists and his enthusiasm for embracing any fatuous argument based on the Human Rights Act. Even Flick found him exasperating.

She said, 'At this time of night we could seek warrants from a justice of the peace. I think we should wake up Mr Murray. He's more practical than the sheriff. There's a fiscal who owes me a favour.' The other two listened, surprised and impressed, as Flick called Harriet Cowan and, gently reminding her of her condition when attending when Montpellier's body had been found, got her to agree to everything she asked. They would meet at Murray's house in City Road in three quarters of an hour. The fiscal firmly declined the offer of a police driver.

The intervening time was spent checking on the SOCOs and discussing everything that had happened, including both Osborne's and Heather Fabroni's assessments of the Jolly Boys. Anticipating a successful application for the warrants, Flick arranged for personnel to carry them out. 'I know it'll be overtime, but the budget will just have to take it. This is no ordinary inquiry and I don't want evidence to be destroyed before we strike. Sir,' she said more than once to the senior officer on the other end of the phone. Eventually she ended the call. 'That was a struggle but he agreed,' she told the others.

'Well done, ma'am,' Lance said. In full detective

inspector mode, she was back in charge of the investigation.

When their car pulled up in front of Murray's house, Baggo said he remembered it from a previous visit.

'At least he won't be playing the bagpipes at this time of night,' Flick said. 'I hope,' she added.

The short, bald justice of the peace answered the door clad in a red tartan dressing gown that was too big for him. He seemed not to mind having his sleep disturbed. He invited them into the room Baggo remembered. From the tartan carpet to the portrait of Robert the Bruce, it screamed Scotland.

'You're the laddie frae Mumbai who likes the skirl o' the pipes,' Murray said to Baggo after Cowan had made the introductions.

'Yes, sir. Well remembered.'

'I'd play you a pibroch, but I guess that's no' why you're here.'

Cowan cleared her throat and explained concisely why the warrants were being sought; although the cross-firing was historic, it was connected to the 1984 murder, and the events of that year were fundamental background to what had gone on over the last few days. Murray put Baggo on oath and he gave a fuller version, making no attempt to put a positive spin on what had happened to Osborne.

It was Flick's turn and she stressed the need for speed. 'This should not have happened but it opens up a promising line of inquiry. I would not have sanctioned what Detective Sergeant Chandavarkar did, but there is no point in throwing the baby out with the bathwater.'

'Aye, you're right there,' Murray said and he signed the warrants. 'Good luck,' he said as he handed them over.

The McPhail, Montpellier, Lightbody and Harkins houses were all to be searched, as well as Lightbody's and Harkins' offices. Flick was allocating teams when her phone rang. It was Austin. She listened then told the other two, 'Osborne's alive and they think he'll pull through. His left lung collapsed. The stab wound was deep and took considerable force. He's sending me a photograph of the knife.'

The photograph came through and showed a slim, slightly curved blade, coated in blood. It was twelve centimetres long, the same length as the bone handle, and two centimetres wide at its broadest point. It had a serrated edge and a sharp tip.

'Now we know what we're looking for,' Flick said.

20

Kevin McPhail answered the door, grey chest hair sprouting above a silk dressing gown, an aggressive expression on his face. 'What rubbish!' he exclaimed when Baggo read out the warrant but reluctantly moved back to allow Baggo and McKellar to enter.

'What is it Kev?' a woman's voice came from upstairs.

'Nothing, Doll. Just these two policemen want to search the house. They won't be long.' Turning to Baggo, he said, 'You'd better not be and you'd better not make a mess. I play golf with your divisional commander and he's going to hear about this.'

At this, his wife came down the stairs. Her lacy, purple negligee did not reach beyond the tops of her thighs and both officers glimpsed skimpy, matching knickers. She had shapely legs. Even if she was more than ten years older, Baggo felt her attraction. But when she opened her mouth to speak, her front teeth reminded him of a rabbit.

'What's it about, Kev?' she asked.

'Nothing, Doll. Someone's made a big mistake.' He brushed a long lock of hair over the top of his head. 'You go back to bed.'

She looked from Baggo to McKellar, shrugged and climbed the stairs, displaying more of her bottom than her husband would have liked.

He scowled. 'Well get on with it.'

First, they looked for wet clothing and found none downstairs. Then they searched the kitchen. They found bone-handled steak knives but there were eight of them, chunkier and shorter than the one in Austin's photograph. Upstairs there was no sign of wet clothing. A room obviously used as a study was uncluttered with no papers, only a computer and, as the cross-firing had taken place in 1984, the warrant did not extend to seizing that. A shelf held a number of black books. McKellar took one down. 'A diary,' he said then went along the shelf until he came to 1984. Baggo at his shoulder, he thumbed through the pages. It recorded appointments rather than a narrative of events. In April there was the first of a series of curious, cryptic entries involving arrows, numbers and initials, M, R and E. These entries continued every week until November when they stopped abruptly. 'Bingo,' Baggo whispered. McPhail had followed them round. His eyes narrowed but he said nothing. Baggo told him that they were seizing the 1984 diary. He affected nonchalance but a little of the arrogance had gone.

'Where were you at ten o' clock this evening?' Baggo asked.

McPhail raised his eyes to the ceiling. 'Where was I at ten o' clock this evening, Doll?' he shouted.

'You know, Kev.' She shouted back then gave a suggestive giggle.

'But the officers don't,' he shouted back.

'You were in bed with me. Do they need to know more?'

'We don't want to shock them, Doll.' He turned to Baggo. 'There's your answer.'

'Did you speak to Mr Lightbody late this afternoon or early this evening?'

He frowned. 'I may have. I don't remember.'

'We can check the phone records.'

He returned Baggo's stare. 'I said, I don't remember.'

'Well maybe I can jog your memory. He may have mentioned cross-firing.'

His eyes flickered. 'What's that?'

'It was a way of fooling a bank that a company was doing good business. It involved the company and someone else swapping cheques for the same amount.'

'I don't remember anything like that.'

'So you say. We'll be in touch, I'm sure.'

'Well try to make it a more civilised time.' He sounded bullish but there was no mention of golf with the divisional commander as the officers left.

* * *

There was a light showing under the fold-up metal door of the Lightbodys' garage when Di Falco and

Gilsland arrived with their search warrant shortly after one o' clock. At least two minutes passed before James Lightbody answered the door. Dressed in light trousers and an open-neck shirt, there was sweat on his forehead and under his arms. 'What can I do for you?' he asked nervously.

Di Falco showed him the warrant, which he scrutinised carefully, giving himself thinking time. 'Are you aware there's a light on in your garage, sir?' Di Falco asked.

His eyes widened in alarm. 'Yes. I was just tidying a few things.'

'Well I think we should start there. After you, sir.'

Visibly shaking, Lightbody led the way through the kitchen and down two steps into the garage. It was packed with a variety of things heaped one on top of others: a wine rack holding several bottles, two step ladders, an armchair, a washing machine, its front to the wall, garden tools, two lawnmowers, one on its side, three different-sized tables, coils of wire, a stereo system, a projector and screen, boxes of slides, a standard lamp, two golf bags, one stuffed with clubs the other empty, two battered suitcases, several jam jars, a tennis racquet, piles of books. It was very dusty and could not have housed a car for years. Lightbody was obviously a hoarder. 'He must have been severely potty-trained,' Gilsland whispered.

But what caught both officers' eye were the brown, cardboard office files, mountains of them, all along one wall. Di Falco picked his way through to them and saw that there was a section where the dust had been disturbed recently. He took a file at random and saw it dated back to 1984. 'We'll have to have a look at these, sir,' he said.

'Fine,' Lightbody said, sitting down on an ottoman.

There was something about the way he did this that made Gilsland curious. 'Perhaps I might look in here first,' he said.

Reluctantly, Lightbody got up. Gilsland opened the ottoman and found several files, all thin. The top one, apparently relating to an address in Anstruther, contained two copy letters, one to East Neuk Properties Ltd enclosing a cheque for twenty-one thousand pounds, the other to Montpelliers, acknowledging receipt of a cheque for the same amount. The letters were dated June 1984.

'Planning to have a bonfire, sir?' Gilsland asked.

'I haven't done anything wrong,' Lightbody spluttered, but his face told a different story.

'Where were you at ten o' clock this evening?' Di Falco asked.

'I was here. Why?'

'A man was injured in South Street. It's an attempted murder. At the moment.'

He took a step back, nearly losing his footing on a roll of carpet. 'I don't know anything about that.'

'The man had called on you at your office this afternoon. What did you discuss?'

His eyes darted round the garage. 'I can't say. Client confidentiality.'

'But he wasn't a client, was he? I believe he talked about cross-firing back in 1984. That's why you were trying to find the files so that you could destroy them.'Lightbody breathed faster. He looked at the floor for inspiration. Di Falco continued, 'Whom did you tell about this man? We can and will get the phone records. It really would be best for you to come clean now. You've already been warned about obstructing the course of justice.'

In a small voice, 'I phoned Kevin McPhail and told him.'

'Yes?'

'He told me to do nothing and tough it out. The man couldn't prove anything, he said. There's a lot of crap on the internet and no one pays attention to it unless there's proof. So I did nothing, well except look out some files.'

'Did you phone anyone else?'

'I thought Georgia should know, as he'd threatened to name Joss. I said I'd phoned Kevin and we were going to do nothing.'

'Did you phone Hugh Harkins?'

'No. There seemed no need. I suppose one of the others may have.'

For the next half-hour, the officers collected files from 1984 and loaded them into their squad car. That done, they searched the house for wet clothing or knives matching the one in Austin's photograph. 'This is ridiculous,' Norma Lightbody, sitting up in bed, protested when they looked into her wardrobe. When asked about her husband she said, 'He's been in that garage of his since supper time. I can't think what all he was doing there.'

Having found nothing more that might be incriminating, they left, warning Lightbody that he would be hearing from them.

* * *

PC Amy Moncrieff parked the squad car she was driving in front of the Montpelliers' house. She was happy to earn overtime as she was due to get married before Christmas and excited to be working with DI Flick Fortune, whom she adored. By contrast, Flick was apprehensive; if these searches did not bring results she would have added the sins of wasting money and upsetting the bereaved to her list of errors.

The house was in darkness and Flick pressed the bell twice, long and hard, before a light came on in the hall. The door was answered by a tall man of about thirty, wearing boxers and a black 'I love NY' tee shirt. He blinked when he saw the two women and looked astonished when Flick identified herself and Moncrieff. When she showed him the search warrant, he blurted out, 'I don't understand.' His accent and bearing were patrician.

'Are you David Montpellier?' Flick asked. She remembered the son was due to come up from London and she could see a resemblance to the dead man.

'Yes. My mother is extremely upset. I trust there is some good reason for this.'

'May we come in please? We'll do what we have to do as quickly and as delicately as we can.'

He stepped aside to let them in. Flick noticed that the TOILET label had been removed from its door. Efficiently, the officers went from room to room. Flick paid particular attention to the study but there was nothing of interest there. In the kitchen they found a set of steak knives which did not have bone handles. In a utility room at the back of the house, a large waterproof jacket with a hood was hanging up to dry. 'We'll have to take this for examination,' Flick told David Montpellier as Moncrieff put it into an evidence bag. 'Were you out this evening?'

'If you must know, I went to the Lammas Fair. I haven't been in St Andrews at this time for years and as a boy I used to enjoy it.'

'Did you walk?'

'Yes. Parking's hopeless.'

'Did your mother go with you?'

'That's ridiculous. No.'

'When did you get back?'

'I don't know. Maybe ten-thirty. Why?'

'There was an incident at the fair tonight. At any point did you run down South Street?'

He screwed up his face. 'No.'

'Were you ever near the Terminator ride?'

'I went right along South Street, so I suppose I probably was. But I can't remember what they called the different rides.'

'Did you go on many?'

'Not really. I went on one that sent me up above the houses in a pod. It was pretty terrifying. After that I kept near the ground, dodgems and things. That was fun. I really don't think I can help you.'

'Did you or your mother speak to Mr Lightbody or Mr McPhail yesterday?'

'I've been fielding the calls. There have been so many. Yes, I think both phoned to check on mother.'

Going upstairs to complete the search, Flick was confronted by Georgia Montpellier on the top landing. She looked awful, her face tear-stained, her hair sticking out wildly. 'Can you not let us mourn in peace?' she wailed. There seemed nothing false about her despair.

'I'm truly sorry but we have to do this,' Flick said, and meant it. 'We'll be as quick as possible.'

While Moncrieff searched Georgia's bedroom, Flick went round the other upstairs rooms. One bedroom was obviously used as a working study, but the papers in it were not unusual and did not go back many years. When the search was over, David showed them out. Both officers could tell that under a cool exterior, he was seething.

'I felt sorry for her,' Amy Moncrieff said as they drove away. 'I bet she normally looks good, very stylish. She must like red. She had a pair of red trousers hanging on a chair in her bedroom and another pair in the laundry basket. They were a bit muddy but not wet, so I didn't seize them.'

At that moment, Flick's phone rang. It was Lance.

In the Harkins' kitchen were five steak knives identical to the one used on Osborne. And hanging up to dry was a man's waterproof jacket. Flick was delighted. 'Bring in Hugh Harkins,' she said. 'Detain him for the attempted murder of Noel Osborne.'

21

Baggo had wanted to be present for the interview but Flick had over-ruled him. Now, in an interview room in Cupar police station, she faced Harkins across a Formica-topped table. She nodded to Lance and he began recording. First, she cautioned Harkins then asked if he wanted a solicitor.

'Not at the moment,' he replied, his left shoulder twitching violently. He looked very angry. This was not a good sign; Flick expected him to be apprehensive.

She placed the five steak knives in front of him and he agreed they were his. When Flick slid Austin's photograph across the table he looked at her with concern. After a pause, he agreed that the knife in the photograph was very similar to his ones. He said he thought he had a set of six; if the knife in the photograph was his, he had no idea when it had been taken from the kitchen drawer.

'Where were you at ten o' clock this evening?'

He frowned then half-smiled. 'I was in Dr Gourlay's house in Hepburn Gardens.'

'Can anyone vouch for that?' Flick asked, fearing the worst.

'Dr Gourlay, Professor Marshall, Wilbur Fry and

Leonard Fitzpatrick. We're a book group.' Gaining confidence from the look on Flick's face, he carried on. 'We met at eight and broke up about ten-thirty. I walked as we enjoy a dram with our literary discussion. That's why the jacket you took was wet.'

'What book were you discussing?'

'*Cold Winter in Bordeaux* by Allan Massie. It's about France in the Second World War. There's a series.'

Flick instinctively knew he was telling the truth. 'What about your wife?' she asked. 'What was she doing?'

'She was at home. Our wives have their own book group and they meet when we do, but in a different house. It's not very PC, I suppose, but it works for us. Last night, tonight, it was Susan's turn to be hostess.'

'And if I were to phone Dr Gourlay, he and his wife will confirm this?'

'I hope you won't feel the need to waken them.'

Flick ended the interview. She wasn't going to release him until she had checked the alibis, but she would wait for a couple of hours before disturbing the doctor.

* * *

While the interview was being set up, Di Falco and Gilsland arrived at the police station with Lightbody's files. While Gilsland worked on Osborne's phone, which Austin had brought over from Dundee, Baggo and Di Falco started comparing the cryptic notes in McPhail's diary with the files. It did not take long to find a correlation. It was also clear that just three parties had been involved in the cross-firing, East Neuk Properties, Montpelliers and Reid and Fanshawe, Lightbody's firm.

'It was a pay-as-you-go phone that sent the text to Osborne,' Gilsland announced. 'There's a surprise.'

At this point, Flick joined them. They could see from the look on her face that the interview had not been a success. She told them what Harkins had said.

Di Falco said, 'They've all got alibis for Osborne's stabbing and for Montpellier's murder, assuming it was a murder. I think we're stuck.'

Baggo said, 'Wait. Did Dr MacGregor not base his estimate of Montpellier's time of death on the stomach contents?'

Flick said, 'Yes. So what?'

Baggo said, 'Osborne said something about Montpellier not remembering if he'd eaten or not. When his wife called him in for supper he said he thought he'd had it. If he really had eaten when he saw Osborne, the time of death would have been half past nine or so, not eleven.'

'Why would she create alibis for the others?' Di Falco asked.

'Maybe she was creating one for herself,' Flick said. 'But when I saw her, she was genuinely grieving, very upset.'

'There was something else that Osborne said

that's niggling me,' Baggo mused. 'Let me think for a moment.'

'Make sure and tell me what it is once you've worked it out,' Flick told him.

Quarter of an hour later, he came to her office. They were alone. 'I believe I know what's happened, but proving it all is going to be a problem. We're going to have to do a trade-off.'

'Tell me,' she said. 'And remember I'm in charge.'

He smiled. 'I hadn't forgotten.' Then he told her.

22

Dawn was breaking as Flick and Baggo parked in front of the Montpelliers' house. It was a better day, dry with clear light in the east, but the front of the house remained dark. To Baggo, who had not been there, it seemed foreboding.

David Montpellier, still in tee shirt and boxers, answered the door and did not try to disguise his anger at being twice disturbed. 'We are here to talk with your mother,' Flick told him. 'It's very important and can't wait.'

He left them in the hall while he went upstairs. They could hear voices but not what was being said. After ten minutes, David came down, now in an open-necked shirt and jeans. 'She'll be with you presently,' he told them and left them in the hall while he disappeared along a corridor. Soon the aroma of coffee made their noses twitch. Flick felt exhausted and wished there was a seat. His adrenaline still flowing, Baggo paced up and down impatiently.

They did not hear her footsteps until she was half way down the stairs. Georgia Montpellier descended slowly and gracefully. She looked magnificent, her posture regal, her hair perfectly in place, immaculately dressed in navy blue trousers and a white shirt with a multi-coloured silk scarf tied loosely round her neck. She stared coldly at the officers. 'The study,' she said simply and led the way.

She made straight for the swivel chair in front of the desk and sat down. Flick took one of the armchairs. Not wanting to be lower than Georgia, Baggo looked round the room before perching on the arm of the other chair. He saw the CD of *Carmen* on the table; there was something of the haughty, defiant matador about Georgia's posture.

'We believe we know what happened, Mrs Montpellier,' Flick said. 'My colleague, Detective Sergeant Chandavarkar, will tell you.'

Georgia raised one black, painted eyebrow and turned an intimidating stare on Baggo. Up close, he noted smudges in the heavy make-up applied, he thought, by an unsteady hand. Her eyes were bloodshot but he saw no fear in them.

'Going back to 1984, your husband was a highly intelligent, larger than life character. He was a successful solicitor and the unofficial leader of the Jolly Boys. He, and you, had an expensive lifestyle. When Kevin McPhail's company got into trouble and the bank was threatening to pull the plug, your husband and James Lightbody helped, no doubt in return for the promise of a share in the profits if they turned things round. What they did was to cross-fire cheques in such a way as to give the bank a false impression of the amount of business the company was doing and its liquidity.

We are now, I believe, in a position to prove this.' Flick nodded. Georgia showed no emotion.

Baggo continued, 'I do not believe you knew anything about this until recently. However Tony Spencer learned about it and I believe he blackmailed your husband. If it had become known what had been going on, your husband's career would have been ruined. He might well have gone to prison. And Tony Spencer was very indiscreet, not a man to entrust with a secret.

'Now when solicitors start doing things they shouldn't they tend to keep doing them. A bit like anyone else. Your husband acted for some wealthy families with trusts. Trustees have to invest trust funds safely, avoiding risk. Some solicitors used trust funds to invest in more adventurous ways, earning bigger rewards so long as they came off. They would return money to the trust with what safe investments would have earned, creaming off the extra profits for themselves. I know this because I have a lot of experience investigating fraud. I bet your husband did a bit of that. The problem for him was that Peter Waldron was moving away from the rest of the Jolly Boys. He was smart, like your husband, but he did things properly and he charged more reasonable fees. But he was a predator. He had already poached good clients from both your husband and Spencer. If he were to take the business of one of the trusts that had been wrongly administered, your husband would be in terrible trouble.

'Your husband's solution was to murder Spencer and frame Waldron. He stole the poisonous frog from Waldron, used it to kill Spencer, then slipped the murder weapon into Waldron's pocket. It worked like a charm. Spencer was dead and Waldron was out of the way.

'Then your husband got dementia. Believe me, I sympathise with you. It must be terrible to watch as the brain of someone you love turns slowly to mush.' Georgia's mouth wobbled but she said nothing.

'Your husband became disinhibited and he was more comfortable with the past than the present. He told you what he had done.' Her eyes narrow with hostility, Georgia glared at Baggo.

'You and he had a position in St Andrews. You were both regarded with respect and sympathy. All that would go if it were to be learned that he was a murderer and that an innocent man had languished in jail for more than thirty years. When, on Friday night, you learned that your husband had told Eric Cox what he had done, you knew you had to act quickly. Cox had a passion for justice and when he got back to his B and B he would be bound to tell Mary Spencer who had really killed Tony. And he would tell the press too.

'You went to the Harkins' kitchen and took a sharp steak knife from a drawer. You and your husband left first and drove along North Street. You found Butt's Wynd, a path that runs from North Street to The Scores, and you waited for Cox to walk past, ready to use the knife to kill him. But then Cameron Smith came on the scene and had a drunken dispute with Cox. Smith knocked Cox out and left. You decided to strangle him as he lay on the ground, far less messy than stabbing him. You took his phone and his wallet to make it look like a mugging.' Georgia sat motionless. Tilting her head back, she looked down her nose at Baggo.

'The next twenty-four hours must have been agony for you. You knew that your husband had no control over his tongue and that it was only a matter of time till he told his secret to someone else. The consequences for both of you would have been horrific. You would both be disgraced and there would no doubt be court hearings about his fitness to stand trial. In addition, I'm sure you will have done your research into how his condition would deteriorate before he finally died. It was a most unpleasant prospect.

'So on Saturday night you gave him his favourite meal with a fine wine, knowing what you planned to do. When Noel Osborne, saying he was a journalist, called unexpectedly it increased your resolve and you took the opportunity to set up an alibi in advance of the murder, for that was what it was. I see you have plenty of crime fiction books and you would know how important stomach contents are in calculating time of death. You pretended that he hadn't eaten when in fact he had. That was a mistake. Unfortunately for you, he remembered that he had eaten and said so. Osborne told me.

'Once darkness was falling you went for a final walk. You would not have wanted to be seen. I expect you took the lane almost opposite your house to get to the Lade Braes. You led him up to the old bridge and pushed him off it. He went head first into the burn, banged his head and probably felt no more. You scrambled down the bank to check that he was dead, perhaps holding his head under water. There was mud on the red trousers still in your laundry basket and I expect it will match the soil from the bank. Cleverly, you changed into a different pair of red trousers before raising the alarm. Particularly as you and your friends gave the others alibis, you hoped it would be put down as a tragic accident.

'There is no doubt that you have been traumatised by your husband's death. You were not ready to lose him but felt that events forced your hand.' Georgia's face was impassive but her eyes filled with tears.

'Yesterday you probably thought you were safe but James Lightbody phoned in a panic, telling you about the online journalist who was about to expose the cross-firing and possibly Spencer's killer. Your son had been fielding calls and you told him what had been happening. Whatever each of you said, he bought a pay-as-you-go phone and texted Osborne. David went to the fair, found Osborne and stabbed him. Between you and Lightbody you would have been able to give a good description. But David left the knife in, another mistake. Osborne, who isn't a journalist but a private investigator employed by

Waldron's family, is expected to live. And we traced the knife back to the Harkins' flat. They have alibis for the stabbing. Two witnesses saw David running from the scene. If we were to put him on an identification parade, I would expect at least one of them to identify him. Eyewitness identification evidence is notoriously unreliable but juries love it. And very often at a parade the suspect's nerves show and make him stand out from the rest. That's not all. If we were to test the wet jacket we took earlier, we might well find minute traces of Osborne's blood on the cuff. Our chances of getting a conviction would be quite good.' Georgia's chin wobbled as she digested this.

Flick had been nodding as Baggo spoke. Now came the important bit, her bit, the bit she was uncomfortable with. 'Our over-riding concern is to get justice for Peter Waldron before he dies and for Eric Cox's mother. If you tell us now and on tape about your husband's confessions to Spencer's murder and then confess to killing Cox and your husband, and plead guilty, we'll treat Osborne's stabbing as unsolved.'

'The alternative being?'

'You go on trial for double murder, David for attempted murder. His life would be ruined. Disgrace for you and your husband either way. If you were to confess, David's reputation wouldn't suffer.'

Georgia said nothing. She turned her chair and reached across the desk for the photograph of her and Joss with David at his graduation. She held it in front of her, seeking guidance from the familiar image, then gently placed it face down as if the memory of that proud day was unbearable. 'Can I trust you?'

'You'll have to. It's by far the better option for you as I think we'll get convictions either way. But I didn't join the police to play dirty. And neither did he.' She looked at Baggo.

Georgia took a deep breath. 'I want to say two things. The idea of murder came from Spencer. He was a nasty bit of work. He and Susan Waldron were lovers and wanted to be together. Peter Waldron loved his wife and Spencer believed he'd never get her to leave Peter for good. Besides, he didn't like Peter. He blackmailed Joss over the cross-firing into helping him to murder Peter. Joss thought out how the murder would be committed. He stole the frog. He was supposed to give it to Spencer, who would poison Peter. Instead, Joss killed Spencer and framed Peter for the reasons you guessed. The cross-firing would never have remained secret with Spencer knowing about it. Joss was desperate. He had to silence Spencer for good. He told me all this about a year ago and I was appalled. This should never have happened to Peter Waldron. He's been in prison all these years. I wanted to do something about it but it seemed too late, somehow. I know that sounds pathetic, but ...' She shrugged.

'The second thing is ...' She gulped back tears. 'I loved my husband and I miss him every second of the day. It was a terrible thing I forced myself to do but, in his prime, he'd have wanted to be dead rather than how he was. And his reputation was important to him. He'd have done almost anything to try to save it. As for David, he was his pride and joy, as he is mine. His future was so important to him. And it is to me. So yes, Detective Inspector, I'll take your deal.'

Flick produced the recording device she had with her, cautioned Georgia and asked if she wanted a solicitor. Then, her voice quavering, Georgia Montpellier began to speak.

23

Later that week, Flick was taking Verity to nursery when she met Amy Smith, who looked away abruptly as she had previously. Then Flick heard a faint 'Inspector Fortune?' and turned.

'I believe I owe you a thank-you.'

'I was only doing my job.' She walked towards Amy. 'Are things settling down?'

'They're good, thanks. My father's new appeal is being fast-tracked and we've heard unofficially that it won't be opposed. So he's delighted, taken a new lease of life.' She smiled. 'He's even talking about doing a Megrahi and living for ages.'

'I'm pleased.'

'And Cammy appreciates being home. He swears he'll never get drunk again.' They both grinned. Hesitantly, Amy asked, 'Would you like to come round for a coffee some time?'

'I'd love to. I'm Flick.'

'Amy.'

Flick felt good as she drove to work. There had been no need to take McKellar's youthful mistake any further and he had decided that he wanted to end his career as he had started, as a constable. The previous day, Di Falco and Gilsland had interviewed Lightbody, who had sung like a canary. He would plead guilty to attempted fraud then the crown would use him as a witness against McPhail; it was an old tactic but it usually worked. At home, she had reclaimed her house, detecting a new respect from her father-in-law. On Saturday, she would have Verity to herself and Fergus could go and play golf.

* * *

The same day, Baggo was driving Melanie to Dundee to see Osborne. He had dropped Charles Arbuthnot in St Andrews to have lunch with his old friend and client. 'Dad thinks you're the best thing since sliced bread, as he would put it,' Melanie told him. This made his heart sing. He resolved to go and see Charles that evening, speak to him alone, ask him … He was determined to marry Melanie but he wanted to do things properly.

He bought some grapes in the hospital shop then they found Osborne, who had been moved to a ward. He smiled when he saw Baggo but frowned when he saw the grapes.

'Take these fucking things away and bring them back once they've been turned into wine,' he growled. Grinning lecherously at Melanie, he added, 'And bring some Viagra while you're at it. Some of these nurses are crackers!'

'Sorry,' Baggo mouthed at Melanie, but she raised her eyes to heaven and smiled.

Acknowledgements

This is a work of fiction and, apart from historical figures and St Andrews stalwarts Julie Lewis and Jude Innes, any resemblance my characters may have to persons living or dead is coincidental. I have, for the purposes of the plot, specified the location of the Montpelliers' house. The property I describe is a product of my imagination and owes nothing to the house actually on the site. I have also opened the new St Andrews Premier Inn a couple of months early. If anyone remembers the time of the Lammas Fair in 2015, I should say that I made the weather fit the plot.

As usual, I am hugely grateful to Annie, my wife, for her encouragement and editorial input. Thanks also to all at Matador. But with any errors the buck stops with me.

We hope you enjoyed this book. Have you read the others in the series? Here are the opening chapters:

MURDER ON PAGE ONE

The body lay on the floor, as warm as the blood that seeped through the plush Wilton carpet or trickled down the white walls.

A clean, deep cut had caused that blood to spurt in spectacular quantities from the left side of the neck until the heart was still.

Glassy-eyed, brain-dead, finished, Lorraine McNeill's high-achieving life was over.

Her black skirt had bunched up round her hips, revealing long, shapely legs – legs to die for. Like a butcher arranging the shop window, the killer lifted a slender ankle and put underneath it a sheet of plain A4 paper. One character had been typed at the foot: the numeral 1.

'Well, you wanted a murder on page one,' the killer whispered, then left to be absorbed into the anonymous crowd.

MURDER ON THE SECOND TEE

The first blow took Hugh Parsley by surprise. It fractured his right temporal bone and tore the middle meningeal artery. He stumbled and fell face down on the grass. A blow to the back of his neck cracked the occipital bone at the base of his skull. He was struck several times about the left temporal area. His brain, penetrated by bony fragments and squeezed by bleeding within the skull, ceased to function. Hugh Parsley was dead.

MURDER IN COURT THREE

'... and you will be hanged by the neck until you are dead.' Speaking quietly, Farquhar Knox QC glared through sepulchral darkness towards the empty dock which, over the years, had held many of Scotland's most notorious criminals. For a moment he wished he had sat as a judge when trials were short and sentences could be for ever. How times had changed. He leaned back in the high-backed leather chair, well-padded for today's softer judges, and checked his fly zip. It was nearly time to go.

He heard a creak to his right and swung round, prepared to bully an intruder into going away. But the blustering tirade died on his lips as the sharp point of an arrow pierced his dinner shirt, entered his torso below the ribs and was pushed up until it penetrated his heart.

A few gurgles were the last sounds Farquhar Knox made. His own day of judgement had arrived.

Ian Simpson was brought up in St Andrews. He lives in Edinburgh.